6 Chelsea Walk

This series is a unique collaboration between three award-winning authors, Adèle Geras, Linda Newbery and Ann Turnbull, all writing about one very special house and the extraordinary girls and women who have lived there throughout history.

This collection first published in the USA in 2019 by Usborne Publishing Ltd.,
Usborne House, 83-85 Saffron Hill, London EC1N 8RT, England. www.usborne.com

A CIP catalogue record for this book is available from the British Library.

JFMAMJJAS ND/19   05772/1   ISBN: 9780794548339 ALB: 9781601304858

Printed in China.

6 Chelsea Walk

1895

Girls
Behind the
Camera

ADÈLE GERAS

USBORNE

For Finn, Colm and Marcella Keating

Contents

6 CHELSEA WALK, 1895

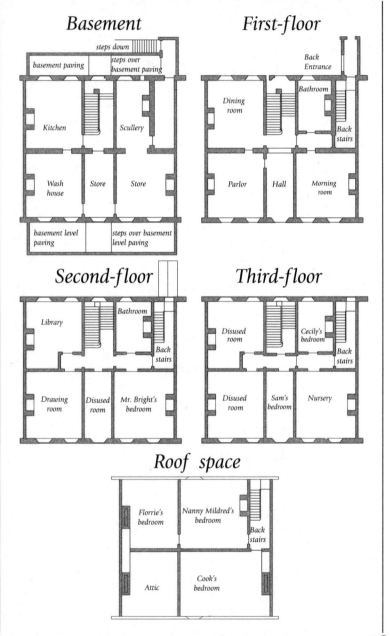

Basement

- steps down
- basement paving
- steps over basement paving
- Kitchen
- Scullery
- Wash house
- Store
- Store
- basement level paving
- steps over basement level paving

First-floor

- Back Entrance
- Dining room
- Bathroom
- Back stairs
- Parlor
- Hall
- Morning room

Second-floor

- Library
- Bathroom
- Back stairs
- Drawing room
- Disused room
- Mr. Bright's bedroom

Third-floor

- Disused room
- Cecily's bedroom
- Back stairs
- Disused room
- Sam's bedroom
- Nursery

Roof space

- Florrie's bedroom
- Nanny Mildred's bedroom
- Back stairs
- Attic
- Cook's bedroom

CHAPTER ONE

Ghosts

Cecily Bright and her friend Amy Chistlehurst had come home from school and were sitting in the nursery of Number Six, Chelsea Walk, talking about whether the house might be haunted.

"I've lived here all my life," said Cecily, "and that's twelve years. Papa was born in this house nearly forty years ago, in 1857, and he's never seen a ghost either."

"Have you asked him?" Amy wanted to know.

"Perhaps he *has* seen one and doesn't want to frighten you by saying so. You say your papa told you it was a school for young ladies more than a hundred years ago… If the house has been lived in for so long, *someone* must have died here during all that time."

"Schoolgirls don't die while they're at school. Or at least, I've never heard of such a thing." Cecily looked away. "But my mother did…she died upstairs in her bedroom."

Amy's eyes widened and she put a hand over her mouth as if she wanted to stop the sound coming out, but it was too late. The dreadful words, the ones she ought never to have uttered, had been spoken.

"I didn't think!" Amy turned scarlet with shame and ran to hug Cecily. "It just slipped out of my mouth before I could stop it…oh, I'm sorry. Will you *ever* forgive me, Cecily? I'm so thoughtless. Please say you're still my friend. I'd hate not to come here and play with you. Imagine if we couldn't see one another whenever we liked! How would I escape my brothers and sisters?"

"You're forgiven," Cecily said. "Though I don't think you should speak that way about your family. You're lucky to have them all. We rattle around in this big house, Papa says. Just him and me and Sam… Since Mama died, it's been very empty and quiet." She smiled at Amy. "I wish there *were* such a thing as a ghost in this house. I wish my mama would come back."

"Only restless spirits return." Amy sounded very sure of herself. "Your mother must be at peace."

Cecily thought that being at peace sounded very pleasant. She herself was always, even at her happiest, aware of the fact that she had no mother and this meant that there was a little grief mixed in with everything she felt. She also knew that Papa was lonely, however much she tried to be a companion to him and no matter how often he told her that he was perfectly content.

John Bright worked as a law clerk, near St. Paul's Cathedral. He had friends with whom he went for walks sometimes, or who occasionally came to Number Six to play cards. He even had what Nanny Mildred called "a lady friend," whose name was Ellen Braithwaite. She was the sister of a colleague of Papa's and whenever Cecily thought of her, she felt her spirits drop. Miss Braithwaite was not unattractive, but not pretty either. She wore clothes in colors that weren't colors at all, in Cecily's opinion: gray and fawn and shades of red and blue that were so dark you could hardly tell them apart from black. Miss Braithwaite wasn't very talkative, nor was she altogether silent. She was of medium height, had light brown hair which she wore done up behind her head in a round bun and was in every way completely unremarkable. She shared Papa's interest in exploration and the study of nature and all the latest scientific discoveries. Whenever she came to the house, they spent a great deal of time in the study, poring over maps and charts and she helped him to arrange and classify his small collection of fossils. Cecily could tell that Miss Braithwaite was devoted to Papa and she feared that Papa might grow used to her and perhaps even fall in love with her and ask her to marry him. She decided to confide in Amy.

"You remember Miss Braithwaite?"

Amy nodded. "I have seen her often and she's just as you describe her."

"I fear she may fall in love with Papa. She might even persuade him to marry her."

"Never!" Amy said. She sounded very confident, and Cecily was relieved. Amy went on: "Miss Ellen Braithwaite sounds extremely dull, as well as looking quite plain. Your papa is far too clever to marry such a person. And my mama says gentlemen like pretty ladies. Miss Braithwaite cannot be called pretty, so there is no need for you to worry."

"But they like the same things."

"One likes the same things as many people and yet one doesn't fall in love with them. Love is..." Amy sought for the right words. "Love is mysterious and unfathomable."

Cecily thought that perhaps her friend was quoting from one of the romances to which Mrs. Chistlehurst was devoted, but she allowed herself to be reassured. She'd dreamed of her father marrying again, and while she'd often imagined the ceremony and had even drawn sketches of the dress she might wear, she was not sure she would be happy if someone else came to live in the house with them. Mama had gone, but if Papa married again, his new bride would certainly want to be their mother, hers and Sam's. That was out of the question, for no one could take Mama's place.

Mary Bright died after Samuel, Cecily's little brother, was born. She fell ill with a fever after the birth and within two days she had gone forever, leaving Papa and Cecily alone with a tiny baby to care for. Aunt Lizzie, who was now Cecily's favorite person in the whole world after Papa and Sam, had taken leave from her work in Sussex, where she was a gardener for a family who lived in a fine mansion. She'd moved in at once to help them. Grandmother Findlay, Mama's mother, traveled to London for her only daughter's funeral, but immediately afterward returned to her chilly house. She was old and infirm now and the Brights rarely went to visit her, in her house near Edinburgh. Cecily found her a difficult person to like, even though she was a relative. When Cecily first met Amy, she realized what a very small family she and Sam had in comparison with other people, though perhaps the Chistlehursts, with their abundance of aunts and uncles and cousins, were a little unusual themselves.

In any case, Aunt Lizzie was the best aunt in the world and Cecily would not have exchanged her for any number of other relatives. She stayed for a few weeks after the funeral and the first thing she did was hire Nanny Mildred to look after the children and be a housekeeper to Papa. Florrie, the nursery maid, was a young girl when she came to help Nanny, and now that Cecily and Sam were a little older, she was a maid of all work. Together with Cook, Nanny and Florrie looked after the house and the family, and Cecily was grateful for their presence.

"Mama was the prettiest person in the world," Cecily told Amy. "When she died, I was only six. That's how old Sam is now, and he seems such a baby still."

Cecily could remember how the house had looked and felt just after Mama's death. What she would never forget – what was still there even now if you knew where to look for it – was the sadness everywhere, which seemed to take up the space that used to be filled with laughter and the sound of happy voices. Papa became suddenly much quieter. He was kind to her even when he must have been as sad as sad himself. She could recall going into the bedroom to see the new baby, when Mama was ill. How pale she'd been! Her skin was almost the same color as the pillows.

Cecily shivered. She said to Amy, "I do know what Mama looked like, of course, but it's becoming harder and harder to remember everything and sometimes I have to look at the picture in the drawing room before I can bring her face to mind."

There was one daguerreotype of her father and her mother on their wedding day in the front parlor. Cecily sometimes stared at this picture, trying to match up her memories of her mother with the pretty, but somehow stiff and formal-looking person in the frame.

"Even when I look at her portrait," she went on, "it's not exactly her. I remember how happy I used to feel when she laughed and played with me and I think of her every night before I go to sleep and then sometimes…"

"Sometimes what?" Amy prompted her friend.

"Nothing. Let's play with the dollhouse."

"But I have to go now, Cecily." Amy sighed. "I promised Mama I would be home early today."

"Then I'll see you at school tomorrow."

Amy ran down the stairs to the front door and Cecily waved from the landing. Then she went into the nursery again. She'd been about to tell Amy that she sometimes imagined she could feel Mama's lips soft on her forehead; her hands smoothing the comforter. And I think I can hear her voice, Cecily told herself, and the songs she used to sing to lull me to sleep. Perhaps it was a good thing she hadn't mentioned that to Amy. It would only have set off more talk of ghosts.

I'm lucky, she thought, that Amy lives next door. The Chistlehursts were the nearest thing to the family in *Little Women* that Cecily had ever met. This book, by Miss Louisa May Alcott, was a great favorite of both girls and Amy had even been named after the Amy in the novel, though she agreed with Cecily that Jo was easily the best of the four March sisters. Amy was, unlike her namesake, the eldest of four children. She was very pretty, like her fictional counterpart, though not as vain. She had no intention of putting a clothes peg on her nose while she slept to improve it and coax it into a more fashionable shape. She was small and dainty, too, and Cecily (who was tall and not at all dainty and had red-gold hair which fell down her back in a riot of curls when it wasn't bound up in braids for school), felt large and awkward next to her. Amy had two younger brothers named Albert and Edmund, and a baby sister named Daisy. It fell to her, she always told Cecily, to look after these little ones far more than was fair.

Amy also had a mother and father who were both alive and well and seemingly happy to live in the untidy and, according to Nanny Mildred, "rather rackety" household next-door to the Brights. Amy and Cecily had met at school and because both of them liked the same subjects and laughed at the same things, they became friends at once. Amy was braver than Cecily, and was also very good at thinking of exciting games to play, which often involved dressing up and acting.

Cecily was crouching on the floor of the nursery, thinking how lucky she was to have such a good friend and happily rearranging the furniture in her dollhouse, when the door flew open and Sam ran in, weeping. She sighed. Cecily couldn't ignore her little brother when he was so distressed. He was making a great deal of noise with his sobbing. Should she remind him of his pocket handkerchief before he dragged his sleeve across his very damp face? Perhaps not. Instead, Cecily stood up and gathered Sam into her arms.

"Stop crying," she said, "and tell me what's happened."

CHAPTER TWO

Mossy is Missing

"Mossy's lost. I've called her and called her and she won't come."

Mossy was Sam's new kitten. Cecily knew that even though the pretty little black and white cat had been a present from their father to Sam at Christmas a few weeks ago, she was the one who was really in charge of Mossy's welfare. Sam loved her, but he sometimes forgot to go down to the kitchen and remind Cook that it was feeding time. Cook said she was far too busy to worry about a cat and whether or not she ate her meals regularly.

"A cat must earn its keep by eating mice," she said, sniffing a little at the inconvenience of having two children getting under her feet. But Cecily knew that no mouse could possibly be as tasty as the morsels of meat from the Sunday roast which she had to cut up into very small pieces. Sam was too young to handle the knife. He didn't mind his sister helping with the care of Mossy, and Cecily had more patience than her brother when it came to sitting still and reading her book quietly whenever the kitten decided that a lap was just the place for a long sleep. And now Sam's darling…her darling, too…was lost.

"When did you last see her?"

"A long time ago. Let's go and look outside. Maybe she's run away down the road. I think she has, Cecily."

"Why do you think that? Mossy doesn't like the cold and there's snow on the ground today."

Sam hung his head and wept even more noisily. "I opened the door. I wanted to go and make a snowball. I think Mossy ran out. I tried to stop her."

"You think? Aren't you sure? Come, Sam, tell me the truth. I won't help you unless you tell me exactly what happened."

Sam *had* let Mossy out. Cecily stood up. There was no way to avoid it. They'd have to go and ask permission from Nanny Mildred to go and look for her.

"Maybe," Sam said, "Mossy's found a door open and run into someplace warm?"

"We'll have to knock at every house and ask if they've seen her. Let's go and tell Nanny and fetch our coats and outdoor shoes."

Nanny Mildred had given the children strict instructions. They weren't to knock too loudly on doors; they were to introduce themselves very politely, say clearly where they lived and ask whether Mossy had been seen. If she had not, then they were allowed to ask whoever they were addressing to keep an eye out for the silly creature. "Silly creature" was what Nanny often called Mossy, and Cecily saw that Sam frowned whenever he heard her say those words.

"And," Nanny added, "you must remember to say *thank you* as you leave. No one likes strange children appearing out of the blue. They might think you were up to mischief. I shouldn't like that. No, indeed. I rely on you, Cecily, to take care of your brother."

"Yes, Nanny," Cecily said. "We'll be very good, I promise." Cecily took her brother's hand as they left Number Six. She noticed that however worried he might have been about Mossy, he still managed to enjoy brushing the piled-up snow from the black iron of the railings near the gate.

The snow had fallen yesterday. It was far too late for such cold weather in Cecily's opinion. February the fifteenth was almost springtime, she thought, but here was the snow, making all the trees sparkle as though white diamonds had been scattered through the branches. The cold, glittering stuff crunched under their boots as they made their way along Chelsea Walk. Usually, whenever they went anywhere together, Sam never stopped talking and asking questions but he was silent now. It was nearly three o'clock and soon the sky, which was already mauve and darkening, would be quite black and the street lights would be on. They had to make sure, Nanny Mildred said, to be back before Papa returned home from work.

Cecily was used to being the person who looked after Sam, and she was careful never to tell anyone how she wished that there was someone to look after her. If we had a mother, she thought, as they peered into every front garden, looking for what might be a kitten's footprints, *she*'d be out here with Sam instead of me. I'd be upstairs in the nursery still, with the da Pontes. Mama had given Cecily the dolls for her sixth birthday and she'd named them all before she died. They were named after the da Ponte family whom Mama and Papa had met while they were on their honeymoon in Venice, before Cecily was born. Mama had told her all about them and even though Cecily had been younger than Sam was now, she remembered every word. The da Pontes were bakers. Papa and Mama da Ponte had a little boy named Paolo and a little girl who was Magdalena, or Maggie for short, and they also had a baby whose name Mama couldn't recall. It had been Mama's idea to call her Bambina. This meant "little girl" in Italian. It was also Mama who suggested that a house for the dolls to live in would be a delightful addition to the nursery, and the wood for making it had arrived in the house before she became ill.

After Mama died, Papa began to make the dollhouse for Cecily. He put it together all by himself, hammering the wood late at night, down in the basement of the house. Then, when it was finished, he brought it upstairs, to the nursery. Cecily had helped her father to decorate each room. She'd chosen the papers for the walls and Papa had cut and pasted them to the wood. There were so many beautiful patterns to choose from and Cecily finally decided on a paper (designed by Mr. Walter Crane, who was a famous artist and wallpaper designer, much admired by Mama) with parakeets and pomegranates on it for the dollhouse drawing room, and one covered in cabbage roses for the bedrooms. The five da Pontes lived there very happily. She'd been about to put Bambina da Ponte into her new cradle when Sam came bursting into the room with the news of Mossy's disappearance.

Cecily wondered whether it was true that because she was twelve, she was too old to be playing with dolls. Twelve, she'd begun to realize, was a strange sort of age to be. Her teachers, her father, Nanny Mildred and every adult she knew didn't seem able to make up their minds about it. Sometimes it was: "Oh, Cecily, you're much too grown up for that," and then "*that*" was things like playing with her dolls, crying too easily when she felt sad, or being frightened to go to sleep without a nightlight. But sometimes it was "No,

Cecily, you're much too young for that!" Then "*that*" became things like, for example, riding on the bus with Amy to visit the Science Museum. You needed a grown-up to go with you…you were too young. You were too young, also, to overhear conversations between adults, though she and Amy had managed to pick up a great deal of information when their elders weren't paying attention. When Amy came to visit, Cecily quite liked arranging the dolls around their dining table and pretending they were grand society folk having dinner parties and love affairs, but Amy soon tired of these games and persuaded her friend to do something more interesting, like playing at ladies and maids. Or practicing writing love letters for when they fell in love, which would be quite soon, she felt sure. Or pasting scraps into a large scrapbook, or writing long plays full of murder and passion and then acting them out. Or, as she had this afternoon, trying to persuade her to go ghost-hunting in the rooms on the third floor of Number Six.

Cecily had never explained to anyone why she loved her dollhouse so much. It had been the one thing that had lifted her grief a little in the days after Mama died. The times that she and Papa had spent together on the floor of the nursery as he put the final touches to the dollhouse were the least terrible times of the terrible days after Mama's funeral. She and Papa used to talk about the dolls. "Look at this armoire," he said one day. "The da Pontes will hang all their fine clothes in it."

"They don't have any fine clothes, Papa. Only what they're wearing."

"Then we'll ask your Aunt Lizzie to make them all the clothes they will need, never fear."

Remembering this, Cecily smiled. Her Aunt Lizzie was Papa's older sister. It was Aunt Lizzie who'd planted the walnut that was now a big tree in the back garden. Cecily liked hearing the story about how ill Papa had been when he was a tiny baby. He'd nearly died and the day that he got better was the very day

Aunt Lizzie noticed that her walnut had put out its first green shoot.

It was their great good fortune, Papa had told Cecily, that they could still live here, in this fine house. It used to belong to Papa and Aunt Lizzie's Uncle Percy, and Papa's Cousin Hugh should have inherited the property after his father's death. But poor Cousin Hugh died himself, in India, of a fever caught while he was climbing a very high mountain looking for a particularly unusual variety of butterfly. Cousin Clara, who'd been a nurse for many years and was now retired and living with her family in Scotland, had no desire to move back to London and Cousin Lucy had gone to live in Italy with her husband, who was a wealthy and aristocratic Italian gentleman. According to Aunt Lizzie, Cousin Lucy would not have considered marrying anyone who wasn't wealthy and aristocratic. And so the house, which was really much too large for Papa and Cecily and Sam, was theirs for as long as they wanted it. Some of the upstairs rooms were closed up, and even though Nanny Mildred said they'd come in useful when visitors came, Aunt Lizzie was the only person who ever stayed overnight, as far as Cecily could tell. The furniture in these rooms was covered in white dust sheets, and Cecily avoided them for the most part. Sometimes, though, when Amy came to play, the two girls opened a door and went in to explore in secret, as they had today. Nanny Mildred would not have been pleased to know about these visits, and Cecily was always relieved when they went back to the nursery.

Aunt Lizzie lived in Sussex, in a small cottage built in the grounds of a large house. She was employed by the architect who had designed the house to oversee the design of the gardens and she found herself working with several under-gardeners who looked after the plants and trees on the property. The Brights went to visit her every summer, taking the train, which was a lovely treat for everyone. Sam was fond of engines and for days before they traveled he would go around the house, chuffing and puffing away to himself, pretending to be a steam locomotive.

Aunt Lizzie could do everything, Cecily often thought. She'd made clothes for the dolls, just as Papa had promised, even if there were not enough of these to fill the armoire. Cecily wrote to her aunt every week, telling her the news from Chelsea and Aunt Lizzie always answered by return mail.

Cecily liked playing with the da Pontes because she was able to make their lives happy. Above all, she could see to it that no one in her dollhouse ever died. Dying, she decided, was simply not allowed. Mama da Ponte was kind and pretty and did all the things that Cecily's mama used to do.

Cecily shivered and pulled her coat more closely around her. How cold it was! Sam didn't seem to notice it, probably because he'd run on ahead of her.

"Come here, Sam," she called out. "We must start looking for poor little Mossy."

CHAPTER THREE

Meeting the Templetons

The two children had knocked on three front doors and asked three different housemaids about Mossy, but no one had seen her. Everybody they met was very kind and promised to look out for her, but Cecily was beginning to wonder whether they'd ever be reunited with their kitten again and she could feel sadness beginning to weigh her down, as though someone had draped a heavy blanket over her shoulders.

Sam was pulling at her skirt. "Look, Cecily," he said suddenly. "Look there! It's that man!"

"Which man? Where?"

"Just beyond the lamppost. There!"

Cecily peered into the mist, which had crept up from the river and was now making it hard to see clearly. "It's Mr. Templeton," she said.

Sam was too young to know his name but he recognized him, of course. Everyone in the street knew Roderick Templeton by sight, and anyone older than Sam also knew who he was. According to Amy (who had the details from Jemima, the Chistlehursts' parlormaid), Mr. Templeton was a very well-known person indeed. He was a painter who specialized in portraits of society ladies, and scenes of town life which showed poor orphans seeking shelter from storms and being comforted by kind benefactors. This part of Chelsea was quite famous for being a home to painters, according to Jemima. There was Mr. James Whistler, for instance, who was an American and also spent a great deal of time in Paris, but nevertheless liked painting pictures of London and lived very close by indeed. Amy and Cecily had seen one of Mr. Templeton's paintings reproduced in a magazine belonging to Amy's father. This was, rather unusually, a picture of a woodland scene and there were some deer in the foreground.

Mr. Templeton was a red-faced man with fuzzy gray mutton-chop whiskers and a loud voice. He always wore a long, dark green cloak over his clothes and a tall hat and because he was a big man, you could see him coming from a long way off and sometimes hear him as well, as he was given to singing snatches of songs from the latest Gilbert and Sullivan operetta. The famous painter lived with his daughter, who was tall and slender and could often be seen striding out in the direction of the river.

Mr. Templeton was approaching his gate. Cecily was just wondering whether she dared go up to him and ask him about Mossy, when he raised his voice and called out to her and Sam.

"Hello! Children! Come here, please. There's nothing to be afraid of!"

Cecily looked around. There were no other children to be seen anywhere. He was talking to them. She took a deep breath and said, "If you please, sir, we're looking for our kitten."

"Aha! I knew it! I knew that two young 'uns wandering like ghosts in the mist could only be searching for something very precious…for example, a kitten."

"Have you seen Mossy?" Sam asked. "She's black and white. She's very small."

"Well, bless my soul, I think I have. I think your search may be over. Just such a creature ran into my house not two hours ago. My daughter has found a basket for the little thing, I believe, and is feeding her with the very best milk a cow has to offer. Come in, come in, and you may take your pet home."

"Thank you, sir!" Cecily was filled with relief. "It's very kind of you to look after Mossy."

"Not at all…and you've saved me the trouble of knocking at every house in the street. This calls for a celebratory cup of something…warm milk, I'd say, for this young man. And perhaps a cup of tea for a grown-up young lady such as yourself."

Mr. Templeton stood aside and gestured to Cecily and Sam to go up the steps to the front door ahead of him. Cecily felt as though she were one of the society ladies Amy had described, on her way to have her portrait painted. One thing was certain: it was impossible to feel nervous or frightened while you were talking to Mr. Templeton. He was a very comforting sort of gentleman.

Cecily was making a mental note of how she would describe Miss Templeton to Amy. Very slender. Tall and with hair so dark and glossy that it shone in the lamplight. At first, she'd not thought her hostess very pretty, but the more she looked, the more she liked Miss Templeton's face. I shall tell Amy she's beautiful,

Cecily decided. I think she is. Her skin is very pale and her eyes are blue. She knew that those words couldn't possibly describe what she was truly like. If only Amy could meet this new acquaintance! Miss Templeton was quite plainly dressed in a brown skirt and a white blouse, with a cameo brooch at the neck, but she'd wrapped herself in a shawl which was the color of the sea: between blue and green and with long fringes on it that moved like fronds of seaweed when she raised her arms.

They were sitting in the front parlor of the house. Cecily was waiting for the cup of tea on the small table beside her to cool down. Sam was on the floor, near the fire, stroking Mossy, who had curled up in the basket Miss Templeton had found for her, blissfully asleep and snoring a little. The parlormaid who'd brought in the tea had also taken some toy soldiers and a kaleidoscope out of a corner cupboard and put them on the hearthrug ready for Sam to play with.

The parlor was so full of furniture and ornaments that it seemed more like a shop than a room in someone's house. You could scarcely see the wallpaper for pictures: portraits, landscapes, watercolors, oils, drawings, all of which, Cecily supposed, must be Mr. Templeton's work. She knew that however hard she tried, she'd never be able to remember everything that was in them. I'll tell Amy, she thought, that they were highly-colored and full of interesting objects and people.

"You're admiring my father's work," Miss Templeton said.

"It's very…" Cecily couldn't think of an appropriate word. She glanced at the mantelpiece, where she could see several photographs in silver frames, grouped around a clock. The photographs were of pretty girls wearing blouses with lacy collars. They had ribbons in their hair and were gazing at the world with soulful looks on their faces.

"I like those," she said, pointing. "They're like real people who're alive and might speak at any moment."

Just then, Mr. Templeton came into the room and

Miss Templeton said, "Why, Papa...this young lady has praised my portraits of Gertie and Maud. She has very good taste, has she not?"

"Nonsense, dear," said Mr. Templeton. "She is – and no offense is intended, young lady, for you cannot help your age – an unsophisticated child. She cannot be expected to appreciate Art at her age. Although it has to be said that with her hair and her height she would have been an excellent model for Mr. Millais, for instance. How would you have liked to lie in a bath and pose for a portrait of Ophelia like Miss Lizzie Siddall? Not a bit comfortable, I would think. But at least done in the cause of Art. One needs a certain training, a certain experience to appreciate painting. There are those who claim...my daughter is one of them...that Mr. Whistler, and even more than him, these Impressionists, as they call themselves...are the coming thing, but I believe in the classical virtues. An *impression* is all very well, but not what one requires from a painting, I feel. There needs to be great skill in imitating nature. And that skill is often only appreciated after much study. One can see all that's in a mere photograph, on the other hand, immediately. It's something that requires neither experience nor great delicacy of understanding."

He sat down and beamed at Cecily. Miss Templeton said, "My dearest papa is the best father in the world, but he is old-fashioned. And not a great admirer of Mr. Whistler and the others. As for photography, it's the art of the future. He's frightened that, very soon, Lady This and the Duchess of That will be summoning me and not him to make portraits of them and his nose will be thoroughly out of joint."

"Rosalind is a fierce fighter in the cause of her craft." Mr. Templeton smiled and took a sip from his teacup. "But *craft*, not art, is what it is and the enthusiasm will pass, I'm sure of it." He turned to his daughter. "You will marry, my dear, and this foolishness, this traipsing here and there carrying baskets of heavy equipment will be forgotten."

"I may marry, Papa," Miss Templeton said, and Cecily noticed that in spite of her calm tone, she was frowning and trying not to sound irritated. "But married or not, I will continue to photograph the world as I see it."

"But why should that be necessary?" Mr. Templeton nearly jumped out of his chair. "The world is all around us. Any one of us may see it and wonder. It takes a painter's art to transform it into something... something more than the ordinary. More than simply what we *see*. And besides," he announced as though he were a magician pulling a rabbit out of a top hat, "all your photographs are black and white and shades of gray and sometimes that brownish color you dignify with the name of 'sepia' but that is not what we see with our eyes. We see an entire spectrum of color... You cannot match a painter for color. Try to deny it."

Cecily opened her mouth to say something and then closed it again. Mr. Templeton was right about the color, but nevertheless... Miss Templeton noticed her and said, "My dear, you want to say something…what is it?"

"I was only going to say that those young ladies will never be seen quite like this again and when they're old this will remind them of how they were…*exactly* how they were…on this one day. When they were young."

Miss Templeton jumped up from the sofa and ran to where Cecily was sitting and took her hand. "You are a very clever girl…you see exactly what I've been trying to tell my father for years. The moment…*that moment*…lives forever. That's it! Exactly."

"Why is my painting not capturing a moment in the same way? Eh? Answer me that, if you can!"

"Because we have no assurance that you haven't tinkered with the reality of the scene before you, for some reason of your own. Some artistic reason." Miss Templeton smiled. "Why, you might decide to change the color of a flower so as to create harmony with someone's dress. You might make it quite different from what it is in real life."

"Real life," said Mr. Templeton, "is not the point. Beauty is the point." He said this with an air of someone who wasn't going to discuss the matter any further and then he turned to Cecily at once and said, "I'm sorry, my dear. We've been so busy revisiting our old battlefields that we've been most remiss about asking your names."

"I'm Cecily Bright," said Cecily. "My brother's name is Samuel. We call him Sam."

"How delightful!" Mr. Templeton beamed. "I was at the theater last night, at the first night of Mr. Oscar Wilde's new play, which is called *The Importance of Being Earnest*. I'm quite sure you've heard of Mr. Wilde...in my opinion, quite the wittiest man in London. And an admirer, I may say, of my work. And in last night's play, one of the heroines was named *Cecily*, just like you! A remarkable coincidence, I call that!"

"Papa," Miss Templeton said, "I think the children should be getting along now. It's almost dark outside and their parents will be wondering where they are."

She turned to Cecily. "I'll take you home directly, but first would you like to visit my studio?"

"Oh, yes, I would love to! Thank you!"

"We must be quite quick then…"

Cecily jumped up from her chair. The clock on the mantelpiece said half past four. "I forgot about the time." She didn't say *because I was enjoying myself so much*, but that was what she meant. "But I would love to see your studio."

"A lot of boxes on stilts up there…strange machines with lenses that you look through and which show you the image upside down! Newfangled nonsense!" This was Mr. Templeton, who had moved to the hearthrug to play soldiers with Sam.

Miss Templeton laughed. "Take no notice, Cecily. Follow me to the third floor. Rather a lot of stairs, I'm afraid, but the light up there is just what I require."

CHAPTER FOUR

A Room Full of Magic

The room that Miss Templeton called her studio took up most of the third floor. It had two enormous windows whose curtains hadn't yet been drawn. Cecily could see a wide expanse of violet sky, and the occasional snowflake drifted across the glass. The room was full of so many interesting things that Cecily could scarcely take them in at once. There were cameras, of course: two of them, one smaller than the other. Miss Templeton said, "That's the one I take about with me when I go outdoors. It's lighter than the big one and takes photographs just as well." Each camera was a brown wooden box, with a concertina-like part on the front of it ("the bellows" Miss Templeton said that was called), and bound with very shiny brass fittings. Cecily could see a tripod, like a set of skinny wooden legs, with a black cloth draped over it.

"I have to cover my head when I'm composing a photograph," Miss Templeton explained, "and when I look through the lens I see my subject upside down, but of course it all comes out the right way up when the photograph is developed. Then, when I'm sure I have the precise image I want, I come out and stand beside the tripod to take the picture. After that, the glass plate needs to be developed in the darkroom. That's in the basement, and it's where I keep my chemicals, too, because Papa hates the smells. How dark or bright the photograph appears depends on the amount of light I allow in through the lens. *Photography* means 'drawing with light'…did you know that? It's from the Greek. I have to dip my photographic plates into all sorts of strange substances to make the picture appear and then soak them in a fixer, which means I can keep the image forever."

"I'd love to see how the photographs are made," Cecily said. Suddenly, she longed to know all about the magical process that could result in pictures that were so lifelike.

"I'll show you another day, Cecily. I'll explain the magic, I promise."

Was Miss Templeton inviting her to visit again? How wonderful! Next time, Cecily resolved, she would bring Amy with her. She looked round the studio, while Miss Templeton picked up various items and put them away into an enormous chest of drawers. "I'm very organized when it comes to my work," she said, "but somehow my studio becomes untidy, in spite of my best efforts."

Leaning against one wall was a huge painting of a garden. It was almost the same height and width as the room itself, and it showed arches with roses growing over them, and a lot of trees and grass in the middle distance and a great deal of blue sky dotted with fluffy white clouds. Set in front of the painting was a bench, and also an urn, and a wicker chair next to a small table covered with a white cloth.

"Ah yes," said Miss Templeton. "I use that as a backdrop. My father painted it for me, which is kind of him, considering how set he is against photography. There are many scenes which I can photograph against that background. For instance, come and sit down for a moment…"

Cecily sat down on the wicker chair, as instructed.

"Now…I had a pretty straw hat somewhere…" Miss Templeton went over to a closet on the other side of the room and opened it. Cecily could see from where she was sitting that it was overflowing with gloves, shoes, scarves and hatboxes. Some garments were hanging up, just as though this were a normal closet in an ordinary house.

"Perfect…" Miss Templeton was pushing back Cecily's hair and she felt she had to say something.

"I'm sorry my hair's so unruly. Nanny Mildred calls it that."

"It's most beautiful…why, half the paintings Papa and his friends admire…the Pre-Raphaelite brotherhood…have ladies in them with hair like yours. Now tuck this rose under the ribbon…there…and we can pretend that you're Mr. Wilde's Cecily."

Miss Templeton picked up a mirror from the top of the chest of drawers so that Cecily could see herself transformed. Then she put it down again next to an untidy heap of jewelry: necklaces, brooches, rings and a tiara.

"You're rather tall for Cecily," Miss Templeton said, "and perhaps rather too slender. You'd be a better Gwendolen, I think. I could dress you very smartly. Gwendolen's a very elegant London lady visiting in the country for the day. If only we had someone to be a pretty country girl, I would compose a scene from *The Importance of Being Earnest*. Cecily in the play turns out to be much cleverer than everyone thinks, of course. It's quite delightful."

"My friend Amy is pretty and dainty," said Cecily, feeling her heart beat a little faster.

"You must bring her here to meet me," said Miss Templeton.

"Oh, I will. She'd love that, I know. Thank you! May we come and see you after school tomorrow?"

"Certainly. That would be excellent. I can think of several poses I might photograph you in. Perhaps some scenes from Shakespeare…or a fairy tale."

She came over to Cecily and took off the hat. "I must walk you back to your house now, my dear, or your parents will think you've been stolen away."

"My papa will not be back from work yet, and my mama is dead."

Cecily blushed. Why had she said that?

"Poor child." Miss Templeton put an arm around Cecily's shoulders. "I'm so, so sorry. Let us go and find your brother. And little Mossy, too."

The three of them, Cecily, Sam and Miss Templeton, made their way back to Number Six in the dark. Miss Templeton was carrying a cat basket. She'd shown Sam where the holes were that would allow Mossy to breathe, because he'd looked very worried to see his kitten shut up in such a small space. When they arrived at the steps that led up to their own front door, Sam ran ahead and lifted the knocker and let it drop.

Florrie answered the door. "Master Sam!" she said. "Thank goodness you're home safe. Nanny and I were about to come and look for you." She took the basket from Miss Templeton. "Thank you, Miss, for bringing the children home."

"We found Mossy!" Sam ran inside, and Florrie followed him. Cecily turned to say goodbye.

"Thank you very much, Miss Templeton."

"*Rosalind,*" said Miss Templeton. "The other's such a mouthful. And we're friends, are we not?"

"Oh, yes!" said Cecily. "And I'll bring Amy to meet you tomorrow."

She watched Miss Templeton walking away into the night. *Rosalind.* A beautiful name for a beautiful person. She couldn't wait to tell Amy all about her.

"Cecily, my dear," said John Bright, "you may come into the drawing room after Sam is in bed, and say good evening to my guests."

Cecily looked up from her pudding. Papa had come into the nursery, as he often did when he returned from work, to talk to her and Sam before bedtime.

"Thank you, Papa..." She was about to tell her father about Mossy's disappearance and their search and how it ended, but Sam began to babble about it in his headlong way so she fell silent. Papa smiled as he listened and looked at Cecily over Sam's head as he gave his son a hug. "I'm sure you'll tell me this story in a more measured way, won't you?"

"Yes, Papa. I will, I promise. Who has come to visit?"

"Mr. Collins, Mr. Drayton and Miss Braithwaite. I daresay we shall play a round of bridge when you've gone up to bed."

He stood up. "Goodnight, Sam…" He kissed the top of Sam's head and left the room.

"Come on, Sam," Cecily said. "*Up the wooden stairs to Bedfordshire…*"

Sam laughed. That was what Florrie always said, and he found it funny. Cecily was happy to see him in such good spirits. She read to Sam every night from his book of nursery rhymes or thought of a story to tell him. He liked adventures with pirates in them and Cecily had no difficulty in inventing tales that he enjoyed. Tonight, she would try to think of a story about Mossy.

CHAPTER FIVE

The Poor da Pontes!

Cecily sat at the table in the nursery, writing a letter to Aunt Lizzie. She sucked the end of her pen and turned the paper over to write a second page.

...and at first we felt a little shy, but Rosalind insisted that she did not wish to be called "Miss Templeton" because that made her seem like one of our teachers, when really she thinks of us as friends. I wish you could meet her, Aunt Lizzie, for she is so interesting and charming.

She is employed in a studio in the West End, as an assistant to a gentleman who takes photographs of families and children and anyone who wants a portrait. Rosalind says that it's very fashionable now, having your portrait taken in a studio. Mr. Templeton says that however fashionable it becomes, there will never be an end to painted portraiture, but Rosalind thinks he says this to raise his own spirits, because fewer people than before are asking him to paint their wives and children.

Cecily sat back, remembering occasions when the atmosphere in the Templeton house became a little heated as Rosalind and her father argued about art and photography. They always ended such disputes with laughter and friendship, but Cecily had noticed how critical Mr. Templeton was of his daughter's efforts and how harshly he sometimes criticized them. Aunt Lizzie would find it all fascinating, she knew. Cecily started writing again.

Everyone wants wedding photographs and christening photographs and love tokens. Rosalind says it's because they wish to preserve happy memories. She says she'll have a studio of her own one day. I wish I could be her assistant, though I haven't told her this. We have now visited her several times since Mossy ran away, and I've watched her composing tableaux: dressing and posing her subjects, and one day I will learn about the darkroom work as well. I've discovered that Rosalind, too, has no mama. Amy's mother told Amy that Mrs. Templeton left the family when her daughter was very young. She went to Germany with a gentleman who was teaching her to play the piano. There was a scandal at the time, Mrs. Chistlehurst says. I wonder whether Rosalind still misses her mama as much as I do mine.

Cecily and Amy were walking home after another visit to the Templetons' house.

"Do you think," Cecily asked, "that Rosalind really means it? When she says she's always happy to see us? Do you think she'd be relieved if we didn't call on her so often?"

Amy stopped walking and turned to face her friend. "Nonsense, Cecily. You are so timid, truly. Rosalind would not invite us to call and give us tea and let us dress up in her jewels and hats if she didn't want us there. I think she looks on our visits as a relief after her work is done."

"Perhaps she'd like to rest a little? Instead of which, there we are, talking to her and getting under her feet."

"If you're so worried about it, why don't you ask her next time? Then you'll know."

Amy quickened her pace, to show Cecily that she was irritated by her remarks. Cecily followed her friend, resolving to do as she suggested. Amy thinks I won't, she thought. She thinks I'm too shy, but I'm not.

Cecily had suddenly realized that morning, looking at the dollhouse in the nursery, that it had been days and days since she and Amy had played with the da Pontes. There was a layer of dust on the miniature furniture and Cecily took the time, before she left the room, to polish the table and the sideboard with a pocket handkerchief. Bambina hadn't been taken out of her cradle for a long time and Paolo and Maggie were lying across the beds as though she'd thrown them there and forgotten about them. Hastily, she'd propped them up at the table and promised herself to play with them as soon as possible.

This neglect was the fault of the photographs. Rosalind had shown them pictures of pretty girls and delightful scenes and though Amy liked these very much, it was Cecily who was particularly enchanted. Amy enjoyed being dressed up as a fairy or a sea nymph, and so did Cecily, but she found herself even more intrigued by the idea of being the person who took the photographs. No one, not even Amy, knew of the secret dream, which she went through every night in bed, before falling asleep. In this fantasy, Rosalind had a studio…in Chelsea, not the West End, for that would mean Cecily wouldn't have to travel so far every day…and all the ladies in the neighborhood flocked to this place to have portraits made of their babies. These little bundles of lace and frills and delicately-knitted blankets would have to be looked after before and after being posed with their proud parents and that would be Cecily's job at first. Then, when she proved herself to be a reliable nursemaid for the infants, she would be allowed to help with other things: ladies and gentlemen posing for engagement pictures; dramatic tableaux of all kinds; wedding photographs…and in the end, Rosalind would turn to her and say: "Oh, I'm a little fatigued this afternoon, Cecily…I shall leave the day's appointments in your hands."

Cecily could hardly see for tears. She couldn't remember when she'd been so upset. She stood up, ran out of the nursery and flew downstairs. Papa was in the hall, saying goodbye to Ellen Braithwaite and a friend named Roland, who had been visiting again, as they did so often.

"Cecily!" Papa said. "Whatever is the matter?"

"It's the da Pontes, Papa… Sam. It must be Sam. And Mossy…he's let Mossy into the nursery even though I've told him over and over again she must be kept away from my dollhouse…"

"Excuse me, please, Ellen…Roland," Papa said. Then he drew Cecily aside and said, "Go to the nursery, my dear. I will say goodbye to our guests and come up at once. I promise. Dry your tears and wait for me."

Cecily sniffed and muttered something inaudible and made her way upstairs again. She opened the nursery door, and sat down at the table, trying hard not to look at the dollhouse.

It's my fault, she thought, as she waited for her father to come up. My fault for not taking proper care of the da Pontes for such a long time. I should have made sure the door was properly closed. Sam didn't mean any harm, but where was Nanny? Downstairs talking to Cook, probably. Surely six years old was grown-up enough to know that if a kitten who was well-known for her friskiness begins to play with dolls, you were supposed to pick her up and remove her from the scene? Cecily was suddenly furious with her little brother…oh, if only he wasn't in bed, how she would scold him! Poor Mossy probably thought that the da Pontes were an unusual breed of mouse!

"Now," said Papa, coming in and going straight over to the dollhouse. "What's happened here?"

"Sam…he and Mossy have been playing in here. Nanny's told him over and over again but he won't listen."

"He's very young, Cecily." Papa had kneeled down beside the house and, picking up the dolls one by one, he placed them on the table in front of Cecily and she burst into tears all over again.

"Look at them, Papa!" Mossy had shredded Mama da Ponte's dress; poor little Paolo's foot had been chewed nearly through and Bambina had been taken out of her cradle and dragged about so violently that her head was almost severed from her body.

"Nothing we cannot mend, Cecily," Papa said, turning the dolls over carefully. He took his daughter's hand across the table. "Do you remember how we finished making the house together? How we looked forward to sticking the wallpaper to the walls? What I remember is how you helped me, Cecily. I couldn't have done it alone, you know. It was such a sad time, was it not?"

Cecily looked up and saw that her father's eyes were bright with tears. She had never seen him crying properly, in the way that she and Sam often cried...of course not. Gentlemen did not weep like that, but his eyes had often been red-rimmed and she could see by the set of his mouth and the stiffness in his body that he was unhappy. Now, the tears were almost there, on his cheeks. She said quickly, "I do remember, Papa. And I know the dolls can be mended, but it was... a shock. And I'm angry with Sam, too. He's in bed, and I can't tell him how angry I am."

"Don't be too hard on him, Cecily. He's young, as I

said. But he probably feels upset about it, too. He may have hidden away in his bed to avoid your anger…"

"I won't shout at him. I'll just tell him to be more careful. May I do that?"

Papa nodded and stood up. "You, too, should be in bed, I'm sure."

"May I ask you something, Papa?" Cecily spoke before she'd thought about it and now that she had, she was nervous about speaking, but there was nothing to be done.

"Certainly, my dear."

"Do you like Miss Braithwaite?"

"What a strange question! Certainly I like her. She is pleasant and kind and we have many things in common. She's a good friend. Why do you ask such a thing?"

"I wondered, that's all," said Cecily. "Goodnight, Papa."

"Goodnight." Papa kissed the top of her head and left the room.

Cecily thought about what her father had said. Pleasant and kind…did that indicate love? She didn't think so, but she intended to ask Amy's opinion again. What was certainly true was that Miss Braithwaite was a frequent visitor to Number Six, Chelsea Walk.

CHAPTER SIX

A Surprise for Cecily

Cecily was writing an account for Aunt Lizzie of what had happened to her dolls.

...I fear you may have to make a new dress for Mama da Ponte. Florrie did a bit of stitching and she's done her best but she is not as good at sewing as you are and it looks mended and patched and horrid. Do you have any pretty material for such a thing? I hope so.

We're already talking about when you next come to see

us. I wish it could be before your birthday, but Papa says the time will fly. I don't think it ever does if you're really waiting for something. It only goes by quickly while you're enjoying yourself. Sam is being especially good whenever he sees me today because he knows that letting Mossy get at the dollhouse was his fault. He is keeping to his room a great deal and being much quieter than usual.

"Cecily! Come here, Cecily!"

That was Sam calling her. Cecily sighed. What was the matter with him now? She'd forgiven him for allowing Mossy to wreak havoc in the dollhouse and he'd been good for some days. Today was Sunday. The Brights had just come back from church, and Cecily had been reading the Lambs' *Tales From Shakespeare*. After lunch, she would write again to Aunt Lizzie about Rosalind's plan to photograph her and Amy as characters from Mr. Shakespeare's plays. At school, she and Amy had enjoyed studying *A Midsummer Night's Dream* and *The Merchant of*

Venice and she'd been consulting Lamb to see what other heroines there were to choose from.

"Quick, Cecily!"

Sam didn't sound in any distress. Rather, he was excited. She ran up the stairs to the third floor and there he was, in the doorway of the back bedroom. Behind him, she could see the furniture shrouded in white sheets.

"Nanny Mildred will scold you for playing up here, Sam. What are you doing?"

"She said I could come. Florrie saw a mouse."

"In here? How could she? The door's always kept shut."

"On the landing. It was there she saw it. It ran under the door. Nanny said to bring Mossy up to hunt the mouse."

"And has she found it?"

"No, but she's in the corner. Maybe the mouse hole's there."

"Why do you need me, Sam? I was busy."

"I wanted you to see…" His voice faded away.

Cecily went in. Mossy was indeed crouched by the far wall, just near the corner, trying to look like a fearsome predator. The baseboard didn't quite meet the floorboards in some places. A mouse could easily have run into one of the gaps in the paneling.

"That's the mouse hole," Sam said.

"How d'you know? Did you see anything run in there?"

"No, but a mouse could fit." He got down on the floor and stretched out next to Mossy.

"Get up this minute, Sam! Your clothes will be filthy and Nanny will blame me for allowing you to lie around in the dust. Get up! You're not going to see a mouse. Neither is Mossy. Any mouse who knows what's good for him will keep well hidden with a cat sitting outside his front door."

"But I see something. Look…" He put two fingers into the hole and pulled out a small square of cardboard.

"Give that to me," Cecily said, and she put it in her

pocket without looking at it. "And now get up and come downstairs. Mossy'll wait for the mouse, and we'll leave the door open just a little so she can come out when she's found him. Aren't you hungry? It's nearly lunchtime, and I'm going to try and clean you up before Nanny sees you."

The promise of food succeeded in luring Sam out of the room.

Later that afternoon, Cecily went to show the piece of cardboard to her father. He had studied the history of the house and knew about the people who had lived here, long ago. She blushed as she handed it over to him, because the picture on it was of a lady with very few clothes on, and indeed, Papa coughed and looked away a little as he told Cecily what he thought it was.

"Here's the date, do you see? 1764… It's a ticket of admission to Ranelagh Gardens, which in those days was a place of entertainment and amusement, just where the park is now. Most interesting…perhaps one of the young ladies who came to school here long ago went to the Gardens, though it's hard to imagine the teachers letting their charges visit such a place. Ah well, it is a message from the past. Perhaps one day I will take it to a meeting of the Local History Society. Most interesting."

He stood up and went to put the cardboard ticket in a drawer, but Cecily said, "Papa, may I keep it? Sam found it, but I would like to put it in my scrapbook."

Her father hesitated, then gave her the ticket. "I'm not sure whether it's quite suitable…this drawing…"

"It was a ticket, Papa, so it must be respectable, surely."

"The eighteenth century was a much laxer time in many ways…"

"Please, Papa…"

"Will you undertake not to show it to anyone?"

"Amy? May I show it to her?"

Papa would relent. He almost always did, when

Cecily looked both eager and anxious. "Very well." He sighed and went to the door. "But only Amy, please. And I hope I may borrow it if I wish?"

"Yes, of course you may. Thank you, Papa."

Cecily stared down at the yellowing card, with its edges worn away a little. It had stayed there, hidden in the paneling for more than a hundred years and now here it was, like a faint whisper from the past and she wondered who the young girl was who must have known Ranelagh Gardens in 1764. Perhaps her ghost might indeed be a visitor to the room. She shivered pleasurably and looked forward to discussing the likelihood of this with Amy.

The next day, after they had left their school things at home, Cecily and Amy went straight to the Templetons' house and upstairs to the studio. While the girls enjoyed the warm milk and buttered scones that Elsie the parlormaid had brought in, they listened to Rosalind telling them of her plans for the afternoon's session.

"I've been considering who you girls might be," she said, "and I think Juliet for you, Amy, from *Romeo and Juliet*, of course. Miranda for you, Cecily, from *The Tempest*. Do you know the play?"

Cecily said, "I've read the story in the Lambs' *Tales*."

"Excellent." Rosalind smiled. "Then you know that she and her father have been shipwrecked on an island, and that gives me an opportunity to suggest the sea behind you...there!"

She uncovered a flat painting of the ocean, with rocks sticking out of a stretch of sand in the foreground. "Here's one of Papa's early landscapes and just the thing, I think. Miranda will be wearing fine clothes, but they'll have been torn and tossed about a little in the storm... The effect I seek is: windswept. Your hair streaming down...wild, untamed."

Cecily didn't feel she could say what she thought, which was: why do I have to be wild and untamed, with torn and windswept clothes? Why can't I be one of the well-dressed heroines, like Juliet or Titania?

It would be rude to complain. I'd rather do what Rosalind suggests, she told herself, than not be photographed at all.

"But let's start with you, Amy. Juliet dressed for the ball at the beginning of the play and leaning over the balcony."

Amy beamed and looked pleased with herself. Cecily could see the white dress, hanging up ready for her to put on, and a beautiful headdress and jewels to go with it. Cecily thought it would have been much more interesting to show Juliet stretched out on her tomb. Anyone knows, she said to herself, that the balcony scene needs Romeo in it. The photograph would be incomplete. She stood up and went to find the velvet cloak that Rosalind had decided she must wear over the torn brocade dress that she'd provided for Miranda.

Cecily watched for what seemed like a very long time while Amy's picture was set up and she tried to follow how Rosalind decided what would make the best picture. She disappeared for several minutes under her cloth and looked through the lens, moving the bellows back and forth, which Cecily knew altered the amount of light that came in through the lens. From her bent-over position she called to Amy to move this way and that. Posed against a flowerpot. Against a door. Leaning over a fragment of a wrought-iron gate that would be perfect, Rosalind said, as a balcony. While she waited, Cecily wondered where the Templetons found the bits and pieces that their house was full of. There were no paintings of the sea nor sections of gate at Number Six. Perhaps that was the difference between artists and ordinary people. When I grow up, she resolved, I will fill my house with all sorts of unusual items.

The photograph was taken at last, and Amy said, "May I go home now, Rosalind? I promised my mama to read stories to the little ones tonight… Will you manage on your own, Cecily?"

"Certainly." Cecily tried not to sound too annoyed.

How typical of Amy to think she was the one in charge, the one without whom nothing could happen. Especially since it was Sam and Cecily who were the first to meet the Templetons! "I am able to find my own front door, I think."

But Amy had already left the room and was on her way downstairs.

Cecily didn't often admit it to herself, but without Amy, she enjoyed Rosalind's company even more. They spent happy minutes arranging the cloak to look particularly windswept.

"Did Miranda not have a mother?" Cecily asked.

"No, she was like you and me… Your poor mama died when you were six, I believe. That must have been terrible."

"How did you know I was six?"

"Amy said something…" Cecily knew that Amy had spoken about her and she felt a little irritated.

"I have no mama either," Rosalind said, "but I was a great deal older when mine left us. She lives abroad.

Papa and I have had to fend for ourselves for many years. Now, stand up straight as though you were looking out to sea."

The subject, Cecily could see, was one that Rosalind didn't wish to speak about. She disappeared behind the camera and was lost under the black cloth till she took the photograph. When they had finished, Cecily began to help with the task of putting the props and costumes away, but just then, there came a knocking at the door. It was Elsie again.

"Elsie, you can see that I'm busy..." Rosalind began.

"I think you should come downstairs, Miss Rosalind," Elsie said. "Mr. John Bright has called for his daughter. I've asked him to wait in the parlor."

CHAPTER SEVEN

Papa is Displeased

"Good afternoon, Mr. Bright," said Rosalind. "I'm sorry to keep you waiting. My name is Rosalind Templeton. I've been photographing Cecily and her friend Amy, too, for a series of pictures I'm composing, based on Shakespeare's heroines."

Cecily was relieved that she was no longer dressed in her costume. She could see that Papa was upset. He'd be polite, she knew, because he'd never met

Rosalind, but she feared that his displeasure might later be directed at her. He said, "Good afternoon, Miss Templeton. I've been concerned about Cecily, not knowing where she was. She is out very late. I was obliged to call on the Chistlehursts. Amy informed me of my daughter's whereabouts."

"I am so sorry," Rosalind said. "We lose ourselves in the work, and then forget to look at the clock. This is entirely my fault."

"I feel that Cecily, too, bears some of the blame. She knows when she has to come home. She has her schoolwork to complete every day, of course."

"Of course. I hope you'll allow the girls to visit me again. They are such good subjects."

"I cannot speak for Amy Chistlehurst, naturally, but Cecily will in future ask my permission whenever she wishes to visit you."

It seemed to Cecily that this meant seeing a great deal less of Rosalind. If Papa allowed her to come, it would certainly not be every day, nor probably, every week. He would think that visiting so often was impolite. He might even try to stop her from coming at all. Perhaps he thought an artist's house was not the sort of place he'd want his daughter to visit.

Papa had calmed down somewhat, Cecily saw, though she feared he was still angry with her. He said, "Thank you, Miss Templeton. Now, Cecily, gather your things together and we will return home."

As soon as they reached Number Six, Papa called Cecily into his study.

"What have you to say for yourself, Cecily?" he asked, looking stern.

"I am very sorry to have made you worry, Papa. I should have been home earlier but forgot the time."

Papa frowned. "I want you to spend more time under this roof and less under the Templetons'. I had a word with Nanny before setting out to find you today and she tells me that you've been visiting almost daily. That must stop."

"But, Papa, did you not like Miss Templeton? Mr. Templeton is a well-known painter. And have you seen the photographs? They are so wonderful!"

"Miss Templeton seemed agreeable. And I did look at the photographs, while I was waiting for you to come down from the studio."

"Did you not think them lovely? Do you not see how lifelike and clear they are? Just as though you were in front of the real person. The camera performs magic."

"I'm the first to agree that the camera is a great step forward in scientific invention and no doubt will have many uses in the future. And Miss Templeton's images are admirable, but that has nothing to do with what I'm saying. Nothing at all. You simply cannot dress yourself up in ridiculous costumes and pose for pictures every afternoon."

"It's not every afternoon that we pose. Indeed, before today, it's been some time since Rosalind took our picture."

"*Rosalind?* She allows you to call her by her Christian name?"

Cecily nodded. "Is that wrong of her, do you think?"

"Perhaps not wrong exactly, but still, it strikes me as a little…Bohemian, perhaps. How many other ladies do you call by their given names? Do you call Miss Braithwaite *Ellen*?"

Cecily shook her head. She couldn't imagine calling Miss Braithwaite anything more personal than *Miss Braithwaite*, however long she knew her.

"Well, then," said Papa. "Do we have an agreement, Cecily? You will not visit without my express permission?"

Cecily nodded and wondered what she could possibly do to change Papa's mind. She resolved to discuss it with Amy at school the next day.

Cecily and Amy sat at the back of the room during Needlework Hour. The pale, April sunshine fell on their backs as they talked quietly together. Miss Perry, their teacher, was a little deaf, which meant her classroom was always filled with the sound of girls whispering to one another while someone's French knots and slip stitches were receiving Miss Perry's full attention.

"Don't worry," Amy said. "He will relent in time. Next time you ask him, he's sure to say you may visit."

"I hope you're right. Today I went to see him again and he said maybe in a little while."

"Well, then…" Amy bent her head to the leaf she was embroidering onto a piece of linen. Her needlework was a little slapdash, Cecily thought and took pleasure in comparing Amy's stitches with her own far neater ones. There weren't many subjects in which she felt confident that her work was as good as her friend's. Amy doesn't mind not visiting the Templetons, Cecily thought. She'd happily forget about Rosalind and the studio and the photographs if it weren't for me. She has her brothers and sisters to think of, and much else to do. Also, she doesn't want to be a photographer when she grows up. She's not like me.

"I think," Amy said, "that you must give him a reason to visit the studio."

"What sort of reason?"

"Well, would he not want his own photograph taken, perhaps?"

"Whatever for?"

"I don't know. To mark some occasion: an engagement, a wedding, a birth."

How tactless of Amy, Cecily thought, to mention engagements and weddings when she knows how much I worry about Miss Braithwaite! But an idea came to Cecily then. She was so happy to have thought of it, so excited to imagine how it might be achieved, that she pricked her finger and had to suck it quickly to prevent a drop of blood from falling on her embroidery.

"It's Aunt Lizzie's birthday next month... I will ask Papa if we might make a family portrait... him and me and Sam and even Mossy... to give her as a gift... Oh, surely, *surely* he'll see that's an excellent idea! She's always been interested in modern inventions, and a woman photographer is something she would heartily approve of. I can't think of anything that would give her more pleasure."

"Wouldn't she prefer a beautiful hat? A pair of white leather gloves, trimmed with beading? A necklace? A ticket to the Savoy Theater?"

"Oh, Amy, you don't know Aunt Lizzie as I do! She is not a white leather gloves kind of person. I promise you, she would treasure a photograph of us." Cecily leaned forward and whispered in Amy's ear. "I fear she had a tragic love affair when she was younger and will never marry now…and never have children. She would have wished to be a mother, I'm sure. And Sam and I are the nearest thing she has to a son and daughter of her own."

"Well, you know your own aunt best, I suppose," said Amy. "Why don't you ask your papa and see what he says?"

For a moment, Cecily imagined Papa laughing at

her idea and being almost as scornful as Amy, but she pushed this thought away and turned to her embroidery again, concentrating instead on a dream of herself, Sam, and Papa with Mossy in a basket, walking along the street toward the Templetons' house.

CHAPTER EIGHT

The Bright Family Portrait

Cecily was telling Aunt Lizzie in a letter how much she missed being able to visit the Templeton house as often as she used to.

Papa should realize, she wrote, *that we learned so much from Rosalind...more than we do in our classes at school. She showed us photographs in periodicals and told us all about the actors and actresses shown in them, performing in Shakespeare's plays. We talked about the*

clothes that the society ladies wear in the illllustrated
papers. We saw pictures of the Queen, too, in a black dress
with a lace collar. And I know a lot about the painters
Mr. Templeton admires and the ones he does not. He is
very rude about someone called James McNeill Whistler
and about Mr. Turner, who lives very close to Chelsea
Walk, but Rosalind admires these gentlemen greatly. She
likes French painters best of all, like Monsieur Cézanne
and Monsieur Monet and Monsieur Degas. Mr. Templeton
sniffed loudly whenever Rosalind mentioned their names.
He called them Impressionists and made it sound like
something no one would ever want to be.

Cecily looked at her father, who was sitting on the end
of her bed. She leaned back against the pillows. "You
said you'd think about it, Papa. What I suggested for
Aunt Lizzie's birthday present. Have you thought?"

"I have, Cecily, and I must say, I am not entirely
convinced it's a good idea. Would Lizzie truly like
such a thing? Or are you simply trying to persuade me

to let you visit Miss Templeton's house again?"

"I *do* want to go back, it's true. You've only given me permission to see her three times since…well, since the day you found me there."

"I don't mean to be unkind, Cecily, but truly, I think you could find more worthwhile activities than dressing up as something or other…what was it last time?"

"Cinderella," Cecily answered. "What's wrong with that?"

She thought back to how they had laughed together, she and Rosalind, while they were arranging and adjusting the rags suitable to the part.

"Do you want to be a clotheshorse?" Papa asked. "A model? It seems a singularly limited ambition."

"No, I should like to be the one taking the photographs. I'm learning from Miss Templeton all the time. Ladies can work in photographic studios. Miss Templeton herself does. And more and more people, Papa, go and have their photographs taken."

"I cannot imagine why."

"Yes, you can, Papa. Think how a photograph reminds you of someone when he or she is not there, with you." She hesitated, wondering whether she dared to mention the daguerreotype of her parents in the parlor. Nothing ventured, nothing gained, she told herself. "For instance…" She hesitated.

"Yes? What did you want to say?"

"I still go and look at Mama's picture every day. It's the only thing that can remind me of how she used to be. Without that portrait, I'd have lost her face forever. Think how dreadful that would be."

Papa stood up and went to kiss Cecily goodnight. "That's quite true. Dear child, you are right. I, too, look at that picture every single day and it *does* bring her back in some small measure."

"Imagine if we had a whole album of photographs of Mama…just as she was. Fixed forever."

"I see her sometimes in my dreams, as clear as clear." Papa was silent for a few moments and Cecily could see that he was thinking carefully about what she'd said. Finally he smiled at her and said, "One *does* forget…and one should not, if that can be helped. You tell your Miss Templeton that we would like to be photographed as a family. I'm willing to pay the normal rate for the sittings, of course. And you're right. Lizzie *will* be enchanted with such a thing as a birthday present and I, too, will be glad of a memento of your childhood, yours and Sam's, when I'm an old man and you're both all grown up. Not to mention a picture of myself in my prime which I can look at when I am gray and infirm and confined to an armchair with a rug over my knees. Goodnight, my dear. Sleep well."

After her father left the room, Cecily noticed that moonlight was coming through the gap in the curtains and filling the room with a silvery light. She got out of bed and went to the window. Looking up, she saw that the moon was almost full and she smiled. The nursery rhyme "Hey diddle diddle" was one of Sam's favorites, and the part about the cow jumping over the moon was nonsense, of course, but Cecily still liked to imagine another sort of world up there, far off in the dark, dark blue…how many miles away? She would ask Papa, who was bound to know the answer. She drew the curtains closed and went back to bed, pulling the covers up around her shoulders. Tomorrow, she'd be able to visit Rosalind again. How fortunate it was that Papa had changed his mind.

"It would be more suitable, I think," Rosalind said, "if I were to come to your house. With family portraits, it's always better to place subjects in a setting they know and feel comfortable in. Not everyone is as willing to pose as you and Amy, you know."

Cecily felt happier than she'd felt for a very long time. She was sitting in the Templetons' parlor. Mr. Templeton was hidden behind his newspaper. She'd just explained to Rosalind about Aunt Lizzie's birthday and how she would be visiting them for the day on May 18th to celebrate.

"If I may call on you on Sunday," Rosalind said, "when your papa is home from his work, then we can discuss which room and what kind of clothes and so forth, and then the following week, I shall bring the camera and all my equipment. Will that suit?"

"I'll ask Papa," Cecily answered.

Mr. Templeton emerged from behind the rustling pages of his newspaper and said, "Your family might consider a portrait...a painted portrait. I would be delighted. Of course, I charge somewhat more than my daughter, but then I have to work much harder and employ far more artistry, to say nothing of skill... craft...call it what you will. All photographers have to do is look and squeeze something and presto, the picture is there!"

"Now, Papa, stop that at once! The picture is not immediately there, as you've said. I have to develop the film. It's a long and quite complicated process. Poor Cecily does not wish to be impolite, I'm sure, so I will point out to you some drawbacks in what you propose. Sam, who is only six, won't be able to pose without moving for sitting after sitting. And then there's the cat, Mossy…"

"The one we rescued?"

"The very same. Now grown quite a bit, I'm sure. Cats, as you know, never do what you want them to."

"Cats are, indeed, altogether uncontrollable. Perhaps you're right. I doubt Mossy will even allow herself to be photographed," said Mr. Templeton, and he sighed loudly in mock distress as he picked up his newspaper again. "Never mind!"

On the day that Rosalind came to call to discuss the photograph of the Bright family, Miss Braithwaite was also visiting, and Cecily wished she was not. She suspected, though she didn't know for certain, that Papa had asked his friend to be there especially, as a kind of protector, because he was a little nervous of Rosalind. This irritated Cecily greatly, and because Amy wasn't there for her to complain to, she fumed inwardly. There were many reasons why she was angry, but the main one was this: Rosalind was almost bound to think that her papa and Miss Braithwaite had an understanding. They did not, she was almost sure of it, though not completely certain. Perhaps, she thought, I should ask him, but what to say? I don't want to put the idea of loving Miss Braithwaite into his head, if it isn't there already. Cecily had seen no real evidence of such feeling, and decided to keep silent on the matter for the moment.

Everyone had gathered in the drawing room, and Miss Braithwaite was pouring the tea that Florrie had just brought in and behaving, Cecily thought, exactly as though she were the mistress of the house. She was wearing a fawn-colored dress with a paisley-patterned shawl over it and Rosalind sitting beside her looked even prettier than usual. *Her* dress was of a shade between violet and blue and had cuffs trimmed with lace. Her hair was twisted up into a complicated arrangement at the back of her head and held in place by a silver clasp. She had a bag at her feet which contained something rather large and Cecily could see Sam eyeing it with interest.

"We're all very excited," Miss Braithwaite said, "about the proposed photographic session. I was photographed once myself, when I was a bridesmaid at a cousin's wedding. One ought to welcome new inventions, I'm sure. It is quite astonishing how lifelike the images are, is it not?"

Cecily felt like screaming. Why was Miss Braithwaite speaking and not Papa, who was surely the one who ought to be having a conversation with Rosalind? Rosalind said, "I have brought with me a portrait I made of Cecily recently…as a gift for the whole family but most of all for you, Cecily."

She reached into her bag and took out something about the same size as a book, but flat. "It's Cecily posing as Miranda, from *The Tempest*."

Papa took the proffered image and Cecily went to stand beside him to have a look.

"Oh!" she said, lost for words. Was this really her? Could it be? Cecily had seen some other photographs that Rosalind had taken of her, and had grown more used to seeing her own image magically transported to a piece of stiff paper. But this portrait was beautiful. She looked quite unlike herself in some ways and very like in others. She was staring toward the edge of the frame. Her hair seemed to be streaming out behind her, because of the skillful way Rosalind had arranged it on the cloak. In the background, the painting of rocks and seashore looked wonderfully lifelike, and Cecily was amazed by the emotions that the expression on her face conveyed: she was sad and full of longing, and looking toward the horizon as though she expected something astonishing to be there, in the distance, almost out of reach. "Thank you!" she added, rather inadequately, and Rosalind smiled at her.

"You are very welcome," she said.

"It's a remarkable portrait, Miss Templeton," said Papa. "I am very grateful and it will have pride of place in the parlor, I promise you. I am more than ever convinced that Cecily's idea of a family portrait as a gift for my sister is a good one."

He placed the photograph on the mantelpiece and Miss Braithwaite made some indistinct noises meant to convey approval. Sam, bored after too many minutes of grown-ups talking, had started to kick the carpet with the toes of his shoes. Cecily said, "May I take Sam to the nursery?"

"An excellent suggestion," Papa replied, and Miss Braithwaite turned to Rosalind and added, "Cecily is so good with her little brother. She's a great help to her father."

Rosalind said, "Sam, dear, I will come up and see your nursery when I've finished talking to your papa. Agreed?"

Sam nodded, then ran to Rosalind and flung his arms around her and kissed her on the cheek.

"Why, Samuel!" Miss Braithwaite said. "I'm sure Miss Templeton doesn't wish to be mauled in that fashion."

Sam said, "What's mauling? I'm kissing Miss Templeton because she's so pretty!"

Laughter followed the children out of the room. "Clever Sam!" Cecily hugged her brother. She felt certain that Miss Braithwaite would not have been pleased by Sam's behavior. She'd visited their house on many occasions and her brother had shown not the slightest interest in kissing her. Cecily didn't think Sam had ever exchanged more than a couple of words with Miss Braithwaite.

"Will Rosalind come and see us?" Sam wanted to know.

"She said she would, so she will," Cecily answered, but part of her worried that she might forget, or else be held fast in the drawing room by Miss Braithwaite. She could not stop thinking of the picture of herself as Miranda. This image pleased her more than any other she had seen, and Rosalind must have liked it too, to choose it for a gift. It occurred to her that perhaps Rosalind had chosen the picture because Miranda, like

Cecily, was motherless. Maybe that was why it was such a successful portrait: because she herself had felt at ease pretending to be that particular heroine.

CHAPTER NINE

Rosalind and the Dollhouse

"And this," said Rosalind, "must be the dining room. How lovely!"

She'd sat down on the carpet to look more carefully at the dollhouse, without giving any thought to what might become of her dress. Cecily knew that Rosalind was careless of her clothes, as her blouses were frequently marked with paint, or a streak of color from one of her props. Once, when Cecily had stared at a pale streak of chalk on the sleeve of one of her garments, Rosalind had smiled and said: "It'll come out in the wash, Cecily...it's of no consequence at all." She'd added, "I never care how I look, only how what I'm looking at looks. That's a great many 'looks' in one sentence, is it not?" and then they'd laughed together.

"This is," she told the children, "a very fine house indeed. Did you say your papa had made it?"

Cecily nodded. "I helped him, too," she said. "I stuck the wallpaper on in most of the rooms. Papa brushed the back of the paper with paste, and I held the pieces against the walls."

"The clothes are so well-made! Who made those?"

"My Aunt Lizzie...the one we're making the portrait for. She's very good with her needle."

Sam held out the toy soldier he was clutching to Cecily. "Can General Bones come and sleep in the dollhouse?" he said.

"He can go in the guest room," said Cecily. "Put him there."

While Sam was settling his general into the empty bed in the guest room, Rosalind said, "If you'd like them, I've some scraps left of a lovely new wallpaper …my bedroom was redecorated last year. It's a pattern from Mr. William Morris's factory called *Willow*…"

"New paper?" Cecily was taken aback. She'd never imagined that anything in the dollhouse would change, but it *was* true that the paper was a little shabby and coming away from the corners in some rooms. How wonderful if her dollhouse could share the same paper as Rosalind's bedroom! She said, "Thank you! I'd love that."

Rosalind wanted to know the names of each and every one of the da Pontes. After Cecily had recited them, she added, "My parents went to Venice on their honeymoon, and the da Pontes were a real family they met there."

Rosalind nodded. "I don't think you ever grow out of dollhouses, do you? I love them, and this one is particularly fine. I had one myself, but it's in the attic now. Such a pity. Perhaps I'll take you up there one day…" She moved Mama da Ponte from her place at the head of the tiny table to an armchair in the drawing room and took Paolo and Maggie into the nursery where she laid them in their beds.

Sam was growing impatient. "Have you finished looking at the dollhouse? I want to go in the garden now."

"Oh, Sam, why the garden? There's nothing for Rosalind to see there," Cecily said. How tiresome little brothers could be! Just as she and Rosalind were beginning to talk about personal matters. She felt that within a few minutes, the subject of her dead mama might have come up and she could have poured out her heart to such a sympathetic listener! Now here was Sam, distracting Rosalind. Perhaps she'd say she had no desire to see anything outdoors.

Cecily stifled a sigh, but before she could say anything more, Rosalind had taken Sam's hand and jumped up, smoothing down her skirt.

"Delightful! Cecily, there's no need for you to come if you'd rather stay here or go back to the drawing room. Sam will show me everything, I'm sure, and we'll be back very soon."

"Very well." Cecily knew that she shouldn't feel jealous of her brother, but she did. Why, she asked herself as they left the nursery, doesn't Rosalind ask me to go as well? Is she tired of my company? Does she like Sam better than she likes me? She kneeled down beside the dollhouse and moved Papa da Ponte out of the kitchen – who had placed him there? – and put him to sit next to his wife. Most of the time, when she played with the dolls, she was soothed by them and they made her feel more cheerful, so why couldn't she concentrate on their lives now? It was, she knew, because she wanted to be down in the garden with Sam and Rosalind and hadn't had the grace to say so when she had the chance.

I can go there now, she thought, and ran to the window. Looking out, she could see most of the lawn.

Sam and Rosalind were under the walnut tree… Sam won't tell Rosalind about Aunt Lizzie and how she'd grown it from a nut, Cecily thought. She made her way quickly downstairs and out of the back door. The sun was shining now, and Cecily put her hand up to shade her eyes from the brightness.

"Sam! Are you climbing? You know you're not allowed to, when Papa isn't there to watch you."

"I am! I can!" Sam cried. Rosalind was looking up at him. He'd clambered onto the lowest branch and had put out a hand to reach for another, slightly higher one. He stretched out, standing on the tips of his toes. He can't do it, Cecily thought, staring at him. If he puts a foot out and tries to get up there, he'll fall. She felt herself turning cold all over. Should she shout at him not to move? Go and stand under the tree? Move to help him? Perhaps if she climbed up too, she could persuade him to come down with her… All this went through her mind in seconds and before she could decide what was best, Sam fell from the tree.

"Oh, oh Sam, dear!" Cecily shouted and began to run to where her brother was lying, very still...too still...on the ground. Before she could reach him, Rosalind was there, cradling the little boy's head in her lap and smoothing his brow.

"Sam?" she said. "Sam, open your eyes, dearest! Come now, where are you hurt?"

"I haven't hurt myself," Sam said and sat up. "My foot's a bit sore, but I'm not a baby." Cecily was so relieved to hear him speaking, and in a voice that sounded quite normal, that she burst into tears. "Cecily's the baby!" Sam said triumphantly.

"She most certainly is not! She was worried about you," Rosalind said. "And so was I. There's nothing broken, I hope?" She began to run her hands over Sam's arms and legs, to check that they were indeed unhurt.

"Papa will be so angry!" Cecily said. "You know you're not allowed to climb the tree when Papa's not here. You know that very well."

"You won't do it again, will you, Sam?" Rosalind leaned down to hear Sam's reply. He was now standing up, looking a little shaken. "I think we ought to go inside, don't you?"

Nanny Mildred appeared at the garden door just then, and bustled as quickly as she could to where Rosalind and Sam were standing. "Have you been up in that tree again, young man?" she said, frowning. "You are naughty, indeed you are! What have I told you about climbing up there? Come along now… come with me to the nursery this minute."

She took Sam's hand and almost dragged him away. He looked back at Rosalind as he went, and waved happily at her.

"Poor Sam!" Rosalind said. "But this walnut tree is so beautiful. Maybe we could pose the family here for your portrait, if the day is fine?"

"Oh, that would be wonderful! I should have thought of that myself. My Aunt Lizzie planted the tree when she was a girl. The year my father was born…"

"How very appropriate! I will consult with your father of course. I think he's expecting an indoor photograph, and we discussed the possibility of his study, but this will be much more…interesting. The light outside…" She examined the tree with renewed interest.

"Sam really likes you, you know," Cecily said. "Look, he's waving to us from the nursery window."

"I'm very pleased he does," Rosalind said, waving back. "He's a lovely child." Cecily said nothing and Rosalind, noticing her silence, put an arm around her shoulders and squeezed her close. "And you, Cecily, are lovely too…you know I think that, do you not?"

Cecily nodded, feeling happiness spread through her as though it were a growing plant. If only Rosalind could stay here forever, she thought. If only we had a mother like her, Sam and I. She thought this, and as she did, an idea came into her mind.

CHAPTER TEN

The Bright Family Photograph

"…and it isn't just me, Amy. Sam thinks almost the same thing, even though I've not spoken to him about it. I know he'd love Rosalind to be our mother."

Cecily and Amy were sitting under the walnut tree in the garden of Number Six, Chelsea Walk. Nanny Mildred had forbidden all climbing among its branches, but as the girls were busily occupied making a daisy chain, and talking about Cecily's latest idea, this was no hardship. Amy said, "But Cecily, it's a ridiculous daydream. Why on earth should Rosalind want to be your mother?"

Cecily decided to ignore the rudeness of her friend's remark, which meant, as far as she could see, that Amy considered being a mother in the Bright household a less than pleasant task. "Why," she said, "anyone would think Sam and I are horrid children. You don't think so, do you, Amy?"

"No, of course I don't, but I'm your friend. Someone who isn't accustomed to you both might have a different opinion. You want your papa to fall in love with Rosalind, don't you? And she with him."

"Yes," Cecily admitted. She imagined her papa and Rosalind, sitting in armchairs beside the fire in the drawing room, with herself and Sam at their feet, and chided herself for her daydream. But Amy's remarks were often double-edged. Cecily didn't know whether to feel relieved that Amy had said she was her friend, or offended because she'd managed to imply that she'd had to grow "accustomed" to Cecily before she became one. She'd also made it sound as though Papa and Rosalind falling in love was so unlikely as to be all but impossible.

Amy continued, "You said Miss Braithwaite was there when Rosalind came to your house?"

Cecily nodded, miserably. "She behaved as if she was the mistress of the house. She poured the tea. She stood at the door to say goodbye to Rosalind when the time came for her to go home. She and Papa stood arm in arm."

"Then all is lost," said Amy, using her fingernails to nip a daisy through its fat stalk. "Rosalind probably thinks Miss Braithwaite is your father's fiancée."

"Then I shall tell her the truth. That Papa and Miss Braithwaite are friends and no more."

"Are you quite sure that they aren't more than friends?"

This made Cecily pause in alarm. "I don't think they are. Papa does not act as though he loves her. Not at all. I am sure I would see something in his manner. Don't people behave…well, not as they usually do… when they're in love? And besides, you were the one who said Miss Braithwaite was too plain for someone to fall in love with."

"I did say that, it's true, but I think I might have been wrong. If you look about you at married people, they are often far from beautiful, aren't they? It's possible," Amy suggested, putting the daisy chain over her head so that it hung down almost to her waist, "that they want to hide their devotion from you. They might want to keep it a secret."

"My papa would never keep a secret from me," Cecily said firmly and Amy smiled.

"You think he wouldn't," she said, "but he would. All grown-ups keep secrets from us. They don't even think of it as keeping secrets. They just say: *we mustn't tell the children* and think they're doing it for our good."

"Stop! You're making me feel gloomy!" Cecily said. "I'm going to try and bring my papa and Rosalind together as much as I can. She's so pretty that he's bound to fall in love with her, don't you think? If he sees her often, he'll get used to her and think of her as a friend."

"I thought you said he was rather cold when he spoke to her."

"He was at first," Cecily said, "but now that she's visited the house, he'll be more cordial, I'm sure."

"But," said Amy, "what will happen if he starts to like *her* better but she will have none of *him*? Perhaps your papa isn't to her taste. Are you certain she hasn't a beau we know nothing about?"

Cecily fell back onto the grass, not caring that there would probably be green marks all over her white blouse and Nanny would scold her and Florrie would make tutting noises as she took it downstairs with the laundry. There were little scraps of blue sky visible through the leaves of the walnut tree and Cecily blinked hard to stop herself from crying. What Amy said must be true. Why had she not realized it herself?

Of course someone as lovely as Rosalind must have any number of young men in pursuit of her...oh, it was so dreadfully disappointing! Rosalind would never become a mother to her and Sam and that was that.

Amy left the garden a little while later and it was only after she'd gone home that something else occurred to Cecily: how did her friend dare to suggest that Papa wouldn't be to Rosalind's taste? Anyone could see that he was handsome and kind and ever so much younger than portly Mr. Chistlehurst, who looked just like Humpty Dumpty, with his bald head and round stomach. So there, Cecily said to herself, knowing that she'd never have spoken out loud if her friend had been there to hear. Amy was probably jealous because Cecily had a father who was far superior in every possible way.

"A little to the left, Cecily, if you please..."

Cecily moved nearer to her father. Rosalind was arranging her and Papa and Sam before taking the family photograph. She had visited the house twice more, since the Sunday when Sam had fallen out of the walnut tree. Rosalind and Papa had talked most pleasantly on each occasion, and Ellen Braithwaite had been absent, which made Cecily feel that perhaps there might be hope for her impossible dream.

They were out in the garden, and fortunately the day was sunny, with high, white clouds drifting across the sky. Rosalind had set up her tripod on the lawn and Cecily noticed that she'd brought her smaller camera with her. A white wrought-iron chair and table had been moved from their usual place beside the trellis to a shady spot under the walnut tree and Papa had been directed to sit down and look as though he were about to drink a pleasant cup of tea in the open air.

"Not," Rosalind told him, "as though you were about to be sentenced by a particularly harsh judge to a very long jail sentence." That had made Papa smile, which was, Cecily knew, exactly what Rosalind had intended. Cecily was behind him, leaning over his right shoulder and Sam was on Papa's left, with Papa's arm around him, which would look delightful and had the added advantage of keeping her young brother in position while the photograph was being taken. Mossy had wandered over to the table to see what was happening, and Cecily wondered whether perhaps composing the photograph might take so long that she'd feel like jumping on the table and would maybe even fall asleep there, but her hopes were in vain. The silly cat, quite unaware of the importance of this picture, decided that more amusement was to be had chasing a stray leaf that was whirling about in the breeze, and off she went in pursuit of it. Well, thought Cecily, she won't be in the family portrait but that can't be helped.

"Now, Sam, stand very still, please," Rosalind said, her voice muffled from her position under the black cloth, and Papa added, "I fear you're asking the impossible, Miss Templeton."

"Please call me *Rosalind*. Miss Templeton sounds like someone's rather strict teacher."

"I feel that would be a little… We hardly know one another."

"On the contrary, I know you very well, Mr. Bright. I always learn a great deal about someone I'm photographing."

Papa was blushing! Cecily could scarcely believe it. Oh, I wish I could tell Amy! she thought. Surely blushing means *something*? It might only have been embarrassment, but there was hope it might be something else, Cecily felt sure.

"That's perfect, Cecily. Now try to look into the camera as though something you like a great deal is there, in the lens… That's right, Sam…some wonderful thing…another cat…a dog…a train."

"Yes, a train!" said Sam and he was on the point of setting out across the lawn making steam-engine noises when Papa, gripping him even more tightly around the shoulders, said, "Do not move, Sam!

Rosalind has said you must be still and we are at her mercy."

"Thank you, Mr. Bright. I'm grateful for your help. Ready?" She emerged from under the black cloth, and slid the film into the camera. "Do not move for a moment," she said and squeezed the bulb to take the photograph.

Cecily became a statue. She gazed into the round darkness of the lens. She tried to imagine what Rosalind was seeing. I wish I could look through the lens and take a picture myself. How strange I must look, upside down! She thought about the occasion, a few days ago when she'd been allowed into the darkroom for the first time. What a magical and mysterious thing it was, to see the picture emerge gradually when the plate was dipped and soaked in the strange-smelling chemicals! Developers, emulsion, fixers... Cecily hadn't been allowed to touch anything, but she looked and looked and tried to keep everything in her mind to think about when she was alone.

Soon, there was a small click and it was all over. Rosalind smiled. "That was lovely. I'm grateful, Mr. Bright, for your cooperation. I will try to make a delightful present for your sister and I will come back soon to show you the finished portrait."

"John, I think," Papa said, taking Rosalind's hand. "If you are not to be Miss Templeton, then I can't be Mr. Bright."

Cecily concentrated on watching her father to see how he appeared and it seemed to her that he was speaking in much warmer tones than he had before. He smiled as he looked at Rosalind. Was he just happy, pleased that the sitting had gone well? Or was his affection growing?

"Very well," said Rosalind. "John it will be."

At that moment, the garden door opened and Miss Braithwaite came across the lawn almost at a run, looking much more animated than she normally did. She started speaking even as she approached the spot where Papa and Rosalind were standing.

"Oh, dear Miss Templeton, how sorry I am that I've missed the sitting! I did so want to be in attendance! I'm mortified that I wasn't here to greet you."

Rosalind murmured an answer, which Cecily didn't hear because she was looking at her father. He had stepped away from Rosalind, as though he was a little ashamed of being caught standing so close to her. Miss Braithwaite was now whispering in Rosalind's ear. Rosalind was frowning. She said, "I'm so sorry... I would need to arrange a special sitting, Miss Braithwaite, for that."

"For what, my dear?" Papa asked.

"Why, John, I have asked whether Miss Templeton might take a photograph of the two of us!"

Cecily felt as though she might faint. Oh, please, she thought. Not that. Anything but that... How could Miss Braithwaite suggest such a thing? What will Papa say? If he says he'd like that, Rosalind will definitely think they have an understanding.

Then Papa said, "We have kept Miss Rosalind for far

too long this afternoon. She must be anxious to return to her own house…perhaps another day."

Thank goodness, Cecily thought, closing her eyes in relief. Thank goodness for that. Next time I see Rosalind alone, I'll tell her that Miss Braithwaite is simply a good friend of the family. And I'll try to find out whether there are any young men calling on Rosalind. She was still wondering whether she could ask her such a thing directly, when Papa and Rosalind and Miss Braithwaite went back into the house together.

CHAPTER ELEVEN

Cecily is Puzzled

Cecily was so excited that she could hardly hold her pen steady and she had already made several blots of ink on the paper. Never mind…

…You will soon be with us, dear Aunt Lizzie! she wrote. *Sam and I are so excited we can hardly bear to wait another two weeks. I have very little to write about because everything I want to tell you is <u>very secret</u> and cannot be revealed…*

Cecily paused, put her pen aside and gazed out of the window. She was looking forward to Aunt Lizzie's visit, but what was the point of writing to her when there was so little she could tell? Several days had gone by since Rosalind took their picture and although Papa had given permission for Cecily to visit the Templetons on two occasions, there had been no opportunity to find out more about whether or not Rosalind had a beau, nor discover what her opinion of Papa was. Cecily had mentioned that Miss Braithwaite was just a friend of the family, but Rosalind seemed eager to change the subject. Meanwhile, Miss Braithwaite visited almost every day, and once or twice she told them when she arrived that she had "passed that nice Mr. Templeton and exchanged a few words with him."

This made Cecily very gloomy. She was quite sure that Mr. Templeton would tell his daughter of these encounters and she would think that Miss Braithwaite was constantly visiting Number Six, Chelsea Walk, which was quite true. Cecily wished she could speak to Rosalind about it all, but was not sure what else she could say.

"Cecily, dear," said Nanny Mildred, sounding flustered as she came into the nursery. "You must come downstairs at once. Miss Templeton is here with the photograph. Please go and find Sam. He's in the garden I believe."

Cecily flew to the open window and saw Sam lying on the grass, trying to tempt Mossy into chasing a stick, when she was intent on hunting butterflies.

"Sam!" she called. "Rosalind's come to show us the photograph. Come inside and see."

He jumped up at once and Cecily turned to leave the nursery. Nanny Mildred shook her head. "Well, really, where are your manners? Calling out of the window like that! If I'd wanted someone to call out of the window, I would have done so myself. You should know better, Cecily. Such behavior is far from ladylike."

"Never mind, Nanny dear!" said Cecily, smiling happily. "I was excited, that's all. Will you come down and look at the photograph?"

"I daresay," said Nanny Mildred, allowing herself to be coaxed into a better mood. "It's a fine thing, this photography. My niece has had a portrait done to mark her engagement… She is going to send me a copy."

"You must show me, Nanny! I would love to see it when it comes."

Papa was sitting at his desk when Cecily went into the study. Sam was holding Rosalind's hand. Rosalind was standing beside Papa and pointing at the photograph.

"Ah, Cecily, come and have a look," said Papa. "It's most astonishing…most unsettling too, to see oneself portrayed like this…fixed on paper forever. And you children too. Come and see. Miss Rosalind has worked wonders with her enchanted box."

Papa had asked for the photograph to be framed. This made the picture look like one of Mr. Templeton's and much more special than many of the photographs Cecily had seen, which were simply mounted on dark gray cardboard. She stared down at the three of them: herself, Papa and Sam. I know Papa and Sam better than anyone, she thought, and myself too, but we look…she couldn't decide how to describe the way they appeared in the image on the desk.

I'm quite pretty, Cecily thought, and she immediately blushed at her own vanity. She had seen herself as Cinderella, as Miranda, as Cecily from Mr. Wilde's play but never before had she looked at a photograph of herself as who she truly was. Her dress seemed to glow with the sunlight that fell on it through the leaves of the walnut tree, and the folds of her skirt were so clear that you felt you could reach in and touch the fabric. Sam was smiling. How happy he looked! His hair fell onto his brow and his eyes were shining. Papa…well, Papa looked very handsome. His hand, resting on the table in front of him, was so lifelike that you felt it had just stopped moving. Rosalind had composed the photograph so that the three of them were framed in an arch of branches and she'd made sure that the shadows made by the sun shining through the leaves fell in such a way that they wouldn't spoil the image. That's the most important part, Cecily thought. Finding the right picture to begin with: the exact right way to remember everything.

"It's lovely!" she said. "Aunt Lizzie will love it."

Papa stood up and said, "Rosalind, I cannot thank you enough. When Cecily came to me with this idea, I was doubtful, I confess. But you have made us all look...well..." He glanced down at his feet and he was, Cecily was glad to see, blushing again. She knew her father was not usually lavish with his praise, but he was clearly very pleased. He went on, "You've made us look very fine, and the tree looks magnificent, which I know will really please my sister. I would be delighted...more than delighted...if you would join us for the party on Lizzie's birthday. You and your father too, of course. May 18th is the day. We will be outdoors, if the weather permits, and I shall present her with this gift. Perhaps, if you wouldn't mind bringing your camera with you, you might photograph my sister, too… Would that spoil the day for you? I don't want you to feel you are working when everyone else is celebrating."

"I never feel that taking photographs is work," Rosalind said, smiling at Papa. "And I like bringing my camera outdoors more than anything. I'm interested in light, you see. I enjoy seeing whether the camera can match the paintbrush when it comes to giving an impression of a scene. I admire the Impressionists very much, as you know, but I think my little wooden box does very well. So thank you…that would be delightful. I must go home now," Rosalind said.

"Then please allow me to accompany you," Papa said.

Cecily could hardly believe her ears. Rosalind had said: *"as you know."* This meant that she'd spoken to Papa already about her tastes in art. When had they spoken? Cecily had heard no such conversation. Was it possible that Rosalind and Papa had had a private talk Cecily knew nothing about? When? How? And now her father was offering to take Rosalind home. Did this mean…could it mean…that they were better friends than Cecily knew? Might they become *even* better friends? Might they… Before she could finish the thought, Sam spoke up, "I want to come too! I want to go with Rosalind and Papa."

"Of course you may come, dear," Rosalind said. "And Cecily too, if you'd like to, though of course I don't really need accompaniment. It is only a short distance to my house, after all."

"Nevertheless, you will have a Bright family escort," said Papa and Cecily realized that he was trying to be lighthearted. She looked to see whether he was hiding his disappointment, but he seemed to be quite cheerful.

Florrie had just closed the door behind them, and they were going down the front steps to the street, when Miss Braithwaite suddenly appeared at the gate.

"Hello, everyone!" she shrilled. "I am a little late,

it seems, for you seem to be on your way somewhere."

"We're taking Rosalind home to her house!" Sam cried and Miss Braithwaite said, "How charming! I'll just join the procession, if I may."

She took Papa's arm and everyone set out toward the Templetons'. Cecily was so angry that she could feel her teeth grinding together. How could Papa and Rosalind ever grow more familiar with one another if Miss Braithwaite made such a show of being his special friend? And how did it happen that she always appeared at exactly the wrong moment? It was enough to make a person weep with frustration. I shall have to talk to Amy about it, she decided.

The next day or two passed very slowly. Amy was in bed with a heavy cold and sore throat and Mrs. Chistlehurst had forbidden all visitors. Cecily didn't mind at first, even though it meant she could not talk about what Rosalind had said (*I love the Impressionists, as you know…*) and what it might mean. How did Papa know such a thing? Cecily didn't want to catch any germs, so she was waiting for Amy to feel well enough for a visit. She spent her time meanwhile drawing at the nursery table and playing with the da Pontes and when the weather was clear, sitting on a cushion under the walnut tree with Mr. Lewis Carroll's book, *Alice's Adventures in Wonderland*.

Now she was standing at the drawing-room window, waiting for Papa to come home. He was late, as he had been yesterday and the day before that, and Cecily supposed that there must be a great deal of work to do at his office. She gazed out into the road, not really looking for him, but wondering if she might see his approach. She noticed two figures in the distance: a man and a woman, walking together. I wish that Papa and Rosalind might walk home like that, she thought, but it seems as if they never will. She hadn't visited the Templetons' house since the photograph had been delivered and she decided that this very evening she would ask Papa for permission.

The couple was coming closer now and she could make out…could it be? Cecily brought her face so close to the window that her breath misted the glass. It was! It was Papa and Rosalind was at his side. He was standing close to her, and now he was taking her hand… and she was saying something to him. Now he'd turned to walk home, and she began to walk in the opposite direction, going toward her house. Where had they come from? Could they have met somewhere and walked to Chelsea together? Had they met by accident? Should she ask Papa when he came in? Or Rosalind? She wished more than anything that Amy was there to talk to. Papa and Rosalind alone together… However the meeting came about, surely it meant *something*?

"I am quite sure," said Cecily. She and Amy were in the Chistlehursts' morning room. Amy had been allowed a visitor at last, but Mrs. Chistlehurst insisted that she stay indoors, even though the weather was lovely. "I know what I saw. He was bending over her hand. I never saw him do that to Miss Braithwaite. And he invited her to Aunt Lizzie's party. And he knew she liked the Impressionists. How did he find that out, if he has never been alone with her? She hasn't spoken about such things when I've been with them."

"He's been calling on her and not telling you," Amy said. "They've probably met at an art gallery and looked at paintings together."

"Then that means he likes her, doesn't it?"

"I think it's very romantic… Perhaps they'll elope."

"That's stupid. Why would they need to elope? No one is stopping them from seeing one another."

"There's Miss Braithwaite, though. Don't forget her."

Cecily buried her face in her hands. "I like forgetting about her, Amy. But why should she make any difference to what Papa does?"

Amy considered. After a while she delivered her verdict. "Perhaps your papa *does* have an understanding with Miss Braithwaite. Indeed, perhaps he's asked her to marry him. Have you thought of that?"

"Oh, no…he'd never…surely he wouldn't? She's so dull. He couldn't. Could he?"

"Yes, he could. And the reason he's not spoken about it to you is because he knows what you think of her…and he's plucking up his courage."

"But what about Rosalind?"

"Rosalind," said Amy triumphantly, "truly *is* just a friend, but your papa is keeping their friendship secret out of consideration for his betrothed, who'd be extremely put out if she found out that he was going to art galleries with another lady. I'm sure I must be right."

What could Cecily say to contradict Amy's version of what was happening? It all seemed to fit the case perfectly, and she wondered what, if anything, she could do to stop her father from making such a mistake. Perhaps she should ask Aunt Lizzie. She was always very sensible, but would she want to be plunged into the depths of this problem right in the midst of her birthday visit?

CHAPTER TWELVE

The Birthday Party

"I see that my birthday weather is going to be perfect," said Aunt Lizzie. She was in the nursery with Cecily and Sam, having been banished from the kitchen by Cook, and asked to stay out of the drawing room while Florrie arranged the flowers which had been delivered very early that morning.

Aunt Lizzie was already dressed for the party. Cecily looked at her as she stood next to Sam by the window and thought that although no one could call her a beauty, and although she was celebrating her fiftieth birthday, she was very handsome: tall and slim and always with a smile on her face. Others (like Amy) might think her complexion had seen too much of the sun, from her work outdoors, but Cecily thought she looked splendid in a periwinkle-blue dress, which had been bought for this day.

The sandwiches, some filled with sliced cucumber and some with poached fresh salmon and all looking dainty with their crusts cut off, were ready in the pantry. The cakes had been baked and were ready on the cake stands, and neighbors had lent the Brights their garden chairs to accommodate the guests. Florrie had enlisted the help of some of the staff from other houses in Chelsea Walk to assist with passing around the food and drink. Twenty visitors were expected and would be arriving very soon. They would have tea and cordials and other refreshments all laid out on a long table that had been set out at the bottom of the garden.

Papa and Aunt Lizzie and the children had eaten lunch at the morning-room table ("Not a proper lunch, but just a stopgap till this afternoon," said Cook) so as not to get in the way. Mossy, who had decided that she did not approve of so much disturbance, disappeared early in the morning and Sam, after a long search, found her in the Mouse Hole Room as he called it: the room where they'd found the antique card hidden behind the paneling. She was curled up on one of the beds, almost invisible in the folds of the dust sheet.

"Lizzie?" Papa came into the nursery. "Are you ready to come down to the drawing room? We have a gift for you, and I should like to give it to you before our guests arrive."

"Certainly," said Aunt Lizzie and Cecily took her hand and pulled her to the door.

"At last!" she said. "Come on, Aunt Lizzie. We've been so longing to show you…"

"I'm not allowed to say yet, am I, Cecily?" That was

Sam and Cecily whirled around immediately and put her hand over her brother's mouth.

"No…oh, no, Sam. Don't utter a squeak."

This made Sam laugh and he started squeaking at once. Cecily wished she'd said something else. She'd spent the last few days impressing on her brother the importance of complete secrecy and silence, but since Aunt Lizzie's arrival last night, she'd made it her business not to leave Sam alone with her even for one moment. He'd been very good so far, but she was determined not to take her eyes off him until the photograph was safely in Aunt Lizzie's hand.

In the drawing room, Papa handed the present to Aunt Lizzie. She looked at it and turned it over once or twice.

"Not a book, I think. And not any kind of plant, I'm quite sure. Perhaps…could it be…?"

"Open it, Aunt Lizzie!" Sam cried. "Open it now."

"Very well." Aunt Lizzie sat down in an armchair and began to unwrap the package. When the photograph was revealed, she gasped and turned bright red and Cecily saw that there were tears standing in her eyes.

"How beautiful! All my loved ones! And under the walnut tree. Oh, it's so wonderful! How…when…you must have…"

Now that the secret was revealed, Sam flung himself at Aunt Lizzie and said, "Rosalind took our photograph. We had to stand so still. And Mossy didn't want to, so she's not in the picture. This is me, can you see? Does it look like me?"

"It looks just like you, dear boy! And like Cecily and you, too, John. I am overwhelmed. Truly. I never expected such an extraordinary gift. I will treasure it forever. And who is Rosalind?"

"She's the photographer who took the picture. Rosalind Templeton. Her father is the well-known painter, Roderick Templeton. She has a very good eye, I think," said Papa. "You will meet both her and her father this afternoon. She wishes to take some photographs of you most particularly, Lizzie."

"Oh, no, I could never…I'm not…"

"Nonsense, Lizzie. I won't hear a word of objection. Have you thought how much we would like an image of you to remind us of what you look like when you're down in Sussex?"

Aunt Lizzie hugged the framed photograph to her bosom. "If you put it like that, I suppose you are right. The day will come when everyone will have photographs at hand of everything they wish to see… It's like magic, is it not? Thank you, all of you. More than I can say."

The afternoon sunshine lay in golden stripes across the lawn. The guests had marveled at the photographic equipment, eaten the food provided, and talked and laughed. Cecily was surprised to be approached by Mr. Templeton, who seemed to be waving his sandwich aloft, as though it were a flag.

"Cecily my dear," he said. "Do you remember how

I met you shortly after attending the first night of Mr. Wilde's play, *The Importance of Being Earnest*? I believe I told you then that one of the heroines was a Cecily, did I not?"

"You did, sir," said Cecily, still puzzled.

"Cucumber sandwiches figure in the play as well… They are quite a feature in their own way, in the very first scene! How remarkable!"

He ambled off across the grass, lost in thought and now eating the sandwich instead of flourishing it above his head. Rosalind was sitting down quite near the house with her camera at her side and Cecily went over to stand next to her.

"I think," Rosalind said, "that you should be the one to take the photograph of your Aunt Lizzie."

"Really? You'd let me do that? Oh, how lovely… I would love to! But is there enough light? It's getting quite late."

"No, the light will be fine. I've seen how interested you are in the process, and you've seen how I work…

I can help you. You'd enjoy taking this photograph, wouldn't you?"

Cecily was speechless and could only nod her head. Rosalind went off to fetch Aunt Lizzie. How wonderfully everything was turning out! Rosalind understood Cecily's longing to be the person behind the camera, the one who saw the image upside down and covered her head to compose the picture and make sure the focus was true and clear. The one who decided which single moment, from all the possible moments at this point in someone's life, should be the one that lasted forever.

"What's this, Cecily?" Aunt Lizzie came over quickly with Rosalind following behind her. "This is the time for that photograph of me that you mentioned? I'm very excited at the prospect...and honored...and *you're* going to take it, I believe. Such a treat!"

"Will you please stand there, Aunt Lizzie? Next to that branch that slants down a little...that's right. You have to be very still."

Cecily let Rosalind cover her head with the cloth.

"When you look through the lens and see something that you think would make a good picture, Cecily, come out and then slide the film in and just squeeze this bulb...so." She put the bulb into Cecily's hand where it felt rubbery and smooth. She did what Rosalind had told her to and peered into the lens and there was Aunt Lizzie, upside down but still recognizable. It was strange, but somehow Cecily could tell how the image would appear when it was the right way up... Aunt Lizzie was smiling. Her face was in shadow, and there were sprinklings of sunshine on her skirt. Were they too bright? Would they spoil the picture? No, that would do very well. She emerged from beneath the cloth and took a deep breath. She slid the film in carefully and squeezed the bulb. There was general applause, and Aunt Lizzie smiled.

"Thank you," she said. "I'll look forward to seeing this picture...very much."

She bent nearer to Cecily and whispered in her ear.

"You look so happy, dearest child."

"I am, I really am, Aunt Lizzie. More than anything, I wish I could be a photographer when I grow up."

"Then I'm sure you will be. I've always believed that if you want something enough, you should try your hardest to achieve it. And those who try hard very often succeed."

Amy ran over to Cecily and asked her how she'd felt, looking at the world from under a stifling black cloth. How can I possibly explain how exciting it was? Cecily asked herself. She didn't have the words to express what she felt, so she only said, "It was strange but I liked it." She wondered how soon it would be before she looked through the camera lens again.

Most of the guests had gone, but a few were still left, sitting on chairs in the shade of the house, chatting with Aunt Lizzie. All the friends she'd known when she lived in Number Six, Chelsea Walk had come and they'd brought every kind of gift, but not one of them (so Aunt Lizzie told Sam, and Cecily had overheard them) was as delightful as the photograph of the Bright family.

Amy and all the Chistlehursts had gone home. So had Mr. Templeton because he was expected at an evening gathering in Mayfair. Miss Braithwaite was hovering near Papa, and Cecily stopped feeling relieved that she'd spent the afternoon speaking to other guests for the most part. Cecily and Sam were now sitting under the walnut tree and Mossy had been tempted out by the smell of the salmon in the sandwiches. She'd found a few morsels on the grass and eaten them, and was now fast asleep on Cecily's lap.

"Try very hard not to move, Cecily and Sam." Rosalind was there, a little to their left, and she had moved up on them so quietly that they hadn't noticed. "I'm going to take a picture of you both as you are now…such lovely patterns of light and shade on your dress, Cecily. This image will be dappled all over with light…just like an Impressionist painting…"

Cecily sat as still as she could. While she was not moving, she noticed that Miss Braithwaite had now attached herself to Papa and was clinging to his arm and leaning against him in a very familiar way. As soon as I can move, Cecily thought, as soon as the photograph is taken, I will go over to them and they will have to separate.

"There," said Rosalind. "You may move now, children."

Cecily got to her feet, but Miss Braithwaite was quicker.

"Miss Templeton," she called out to Rosalind. "Please allow me to thank you so much for coming and marking the occasion with your truly wonderful photographs. John, dearest, I've been thinking. Perhaps we can have a picture taken of the three of us, while Miss Templeton is here…you and Lizzie and me. I am, after all, almost a member of the family, am I not?"

Papa looked shocked, but said nothing. Rosalind,

Cecily saw, turned very pale. She said, "I would like nothing better, but alas, I have not brought enough supplies… I can only carry a limited amount with me. I'm so sorry. I used my last plate taking the photograph of the children."

"Never mind," said Miss Braithwaite. "There will be another occasion. Perhaps an even happier one than this, I daresay."

She means a wedding, Cecily realized. Does she? Is that what she means? How could that be?

Rosalind said, "I have to go home now. I'm late already. I'll say goodbye to all of you and thank you for a very pleasant afternoon."

She began to pack up her equipment hastily. Papa was moving to go with her to the front door, but Miss Braithwaite was there before him.

"I'll show Miss Templeton out, John. You have your other guests to attend to."

"You don't need to accompany me, thank you, Miss Braithwaite," said Rosalind. "I will do very well alone."

She was gone so quickly that neither Miss Braithwaite nor Papa could keep up with her. Cecily felt a shadow fall over the whole afternoon.

CHAPTER THIRTEEN

Telling Aunt Lizzie

Aunt Lizzie sat down at the end of Cecily's bed. "I think," she said, "that you should tell me what's wrong. I can see you're not as happy as you were earlier this morning. Has something happened? Did you perhaps have a disagreement with your friend Amy during the party?"

Cecily said, "No, it's not that... It's only..." She didn't know what to say next. Perhaps she ought to keep quiet? But how wonderful it would be to tell someone of her fears and hopes!

"Will you promise not to tell Papa? Promise?"

"I can't promise that, Cecily, but I won't tell him unless I consider it absolutely necessary for him to know. Do you think it will be?"

"No... It's not anything that I couldn't say to him, but..."

"I know. Sometimes it's difficult to talk to those who are closest to you..."

Cecily spoke in a rush because she knew that if she hesitated, she would say nothing at all. "I think Miss Braithwaite wants to be our new mama. I think Papa's going to ask her to marry him, and I don't like her and don't want her to live with us. I'd rather have no mother at all, truly. And I hoped that..."

"Yes? What did you hope?"

Could she confess to what she had longed for? Cecily took a deep breath and went on, "I hoped that perhaps Rosalind... Well, she would be a wonderful mother and Sam really likes her and so do I."

"But what about John? Does he like her? Is she more than an acquaintance? He hasn't spoken of her to me."

"I don't know. I saw them standing together in the street, once. Papa has said nothing about her and meanwhile, Miss Braithwaite is constantly here and today…"

Aunt Lizzie stood up. "Go to sleep now, Cecily. I'll speak to John. I shan't say we've had this conversation. And I confess – though now it's your turn to promise not to breathe a word – I've never had a good opinion of Miss Braithwaite. She is pleasant enough but rather tiresome in many ways. Goodnight, Cecily. I shall have to return to Sussex very early in the morning, so I'll say goodbye, too. It's been my best birthday yet. And I look forward to seeing your photograph of me. It will bring back very happy memories." She kissed Cecily on the forehead and said, "Sleep well."

Cecily did not sleep well. She didn't sleep at all for what seemed like a very long time. The grandfather clock on the second-floor landing ticked away the hours and she heard it striking ten o'clock as she lay in her bed, wide awake. She felt warm and pushed back the covers and went to stand at the window. There was a carriage waiting at the gate of Number Six. Someone was speaking in the hall downstairs. Papa was saying goodbye to whoever had ordered the carriage to take them home. Only one person would stay so late…Miss Braithwaite of course. Perhaps, Cecily thought miserably, they've been discussing their wedding plans. If they marry, I will ask to go and live in Sussex with Aunt Lizzie. Would she have me? But what about Sam? I can't leave him, and school and Amy and Papa and everything I know…and I don't want to leave Rosalind.

She crept out onto the landing and went down a few steps so that she had a view of the hall below. Yes, there was Papa and there was Miss Braithwaite, but she was sniffing and holding a handkerchief up to her eyes. Her voice, when she spoke, drifted up to where Cecily was sitting, crouched just below the turn of the stairs and out of sight. I'm eavesdropping, she thought, and felt a little ashamed of herself but not ashamed enough to go back to her room. She listened as hard as she could.

"I was *not* deceiving myself, John," Miss Braithwaite said. "I had every cause for my expectations."

"But I've said nothing." Papa sounded indignant.

"You had no need to say anything. I *knew*. I was such a frequent visitor. We did so much together. You have always been kind and courteous to me. We have so much in common, John. There was no need for you to say the words. I took them for granted."

"Then forgive me, Ellen. You should not have done so. I have never, not once, said I loved you."

"Ah, but can you say you *don't* love me? In all honesty?"

Papa sighed. "I don't love you, Ellen. I'm so sorry…"

"Sorry! I should think so! But sorry doesn't help me. Oh, how will I live? What will I do?"

Miss Braithwaite was wailing now, and wiping away a fresh flood of tears. Cecily tried to feel sorry for her, but she was so happy on her own account that she didn't have any room in her head and heart for kindly feelings toward poor Miss Braithwaite. Papa was consoling her as best he could, while guiding her toward the front door and her carriage.

"We will still be friends," he said to her. "I like you enormously, Ellen, as you must know. I hope you will feel able to visit us sometimes."

"Never!" Miss Braithwaite swept out of the door. "Never again! Farewell forever, John. I trust you will be happy all alone in this cavernous house." And she was gone and Cecily watched Papa close the door behind her and lean against it, looking exhausted and pale. She crept back to her bedroom and lay in bed, staring at the ceiling. Tomorrow, she thought, I must go and visit Rosalind and tell her Miss Braithwaite is gone. Forever.

Just before she drifted into sleep, she thought: how did Miss Braithwaite dare to call this beautiful house "cavernous"? What a foolish person she is! We shall all be much happier now she's gone.

CHAPTER FOURTEEN

In the Nick of Time

The following morning, Cecily asked permission from Nanny to go and visit the Templetons. She was all ready with stories of how very urgent this visit was, and how she simply had to go, but Nanny was so preoccupied with setting the house in order after the party that she gave her permission at once. Cecily left the house quickly before she could change her mind, and ran to the Templetons' house where she knocked at the door rather more loudly than she'd intended. When Elsie opened it, Cecily asked to speak to Miss Rosalind, urgently.

"Miss Rosalind is packing," said Elsie.

Cecily was silent for a moment. "Why? I mean, please forgive me, but why is she packing?"

"She's going abroad."

"She never told me. She never said anything. Are you quite sure?"

Elsie sighed and stood back from the door. "You'd better come in, Miss Cecily," she said. "You look as though you've lost a sixpence and found a farthing."

"May I see her?"

"I'll ask. You wait here for a moment."

Cecily watched Elsie making her way upstairs and bit her lip to prevent herself from crying. If Rosalind was going abroad so suddenly, there must be a reason. Or maybe she'd been planning the trip for a long time. Cecily pondered this possibility and decided it was impossible. There would have been many opportunities for Rosalind to have said something. Only the other day, she'd been speaking about Venice, and telling Cecily she'd make a good Portia from *The Merchant of Venice*. She would have mentioned it. It looked as though Rosalind was running away, and Cecily wondered whether her flight could have anything to do with Papa. Cecily thought that it must have been the hint about wedding photographs that had upset Rosalind, but surely she couldn't be thinking that Papa was really going to marry Miss Braithwaite? Rosalind must have noticed before how Miss Braithwaite always behaved as though she were already mistress of Number Six, Chelsea Walk, and she knew Miss Braithwaite would be invited to the party, so what must have upset her so much was her belief that Papa was considering an engagement and a wedding. It's lucky that I've come to tell her what Papa said to Miss Braithwaite last night, Cecily thought. I'll let her know that I heard him making it quite clear that he had no intention in the world of ever, ever marrying

Miss Braithwaite and moreover, had never loved her.

"Cecily!" Rosalind came across the hall to her and took both her hands and squeezed them. "Come into the parlor."

Cecily sat in one of the armchairs near the window. Rosalind stood at the mantelpiece. There were violet shadows under her eyes as though she had not slept well. She said, "I'm sorry I said nothing to you yesterday…I was not sure of my plans."

"Did you know you were going abroad?"

"No…no it was something of an impulse. I suddenly felt I wanted to be…well, not here in London, at any rate."

"When will you come back?"

"I don't know. So much depends on…well, never mind."

Cecily had been wondering on her way to the Templeton house how she ought to tell Rosalind about Miss Braithwaite's departure. Should she admit that she had seen Rosalind and Papa together? Should she mention that both she and Sam would be happy to have her as a mother? No, she decided. I'll simply tell her what happened. She said, "Miss Braithwaite won't be visiting us again, I think. She and Papa had a quarrel last night. She told him that she thought he wanted to marry her. She said that she thought he loved her. But he doesn't. He told her so. She was most upset and left in a carriage. She was crying."

Rosalind turned even whiter than she was before, and then her face flushed scarlet. She brought her hand to her mouth and bit her knuckles. She said, "How do you know this? Were you there?"

"I was on the stairs. I couldn't sleep. I went to see who was making such a noise so late at night."

"Did you hear him say that? That he didn't love her?"

"Yes. Yes, I did."

Rosalind sank on to the sofa and tears came to her eyes. "Oh, Cecily…I'm so sorry. I'm behaving like a schoolgirl. I can't help it. I gave up hope yesterday in spite of everything."

"Hope of what?"

"I shouldn't tell you. Your papa said…he said it ought to come from him, but now that you've told me this…"

"I saw you and Papa in the road. Amy said perhaps you'd been to an art gallery together."

"We have met…well, on several occasions since he came to this house when I was photographing you. But there was always Miss Braithwaite in the background."

Cecily's heart began to beat a little faster. "Has…have you and Papa…did you say anything…?"

"No, no, child." Rosalind smiled. "We have discussed many things but not our feelings. He's said nothing that might…well, that might lead me to have any expectations. And then yesterday, with Miss Braithwaite hinting about marriage, I could bear it no longer. I felt I had to go…get far away from everything here."

Cecily looked down at her shoes. What did it all mean? Why had Papa not said anything in the least romantic to Rosalind when they'd been together? *I'll* say something, she decided. I'll tell Rosalind. She said, "Sam and I would be so happy if you were our mama. I wish Papa might have fallen in love with you and married you and then we might all have lived together in our house and been happy."

"Oh, Cecily!" Rosalind buried her head in her hands. "I've wished for that too… I fear it will not happen now, for surely a gentleman would have made his feelings known and his intentions clear before now. Even with Miss Braithwaite still on the scene. There were many times when he could have spoken and still he said nothing, though he must have known… Never mind. It's too late now."

"But it's not too late! You don't have to go abroad. You could stay and find out for yourself… You could go and ask him, face-to-face."

"Oh, never. I could never do such a thing. What would he think of me, if such thoughts have never been in his mind?"

"But there's no one else. I told you what he said to

Miss Braithwaite. He doesn't love her. He said so clear as clear."

"Just because he doesn't love her, it doesn't necessarily mean he has…well, tender feelings for me. I'm sure that if he had, he would have found a way to tell me, in spite of all Miss Braithwaite's schemes."

"Papa is a very quiet person," Cecily said. "He doesn't do things rashly, or without thinking about them for a very long time. Perhaps he thinks you don't share his feelings."

Rosalind thought about this for a moment. "That's possible, I suppose, though I did think that I…well, never mind. I will recover from my disappointment while I'm abroad and when I return, I am sure we'll still be friends, will we not?"

"You're determined to go? You won't change your mind?" It was Cecily's turn to blink her eyes to stop herself from crying.

"I must… Kiss me goodbye, Cecily, and make sure to give Sam a hug from me."

"He'll be so sad…we both will."

"I know and so will I…but it can't be helped."

Rosalind went with Cecily to the front door. They clung together on the doorstep and then Cecily went down the steps to the street and started to walk home. Why hadn't Rosalind believed her? She was obviously not entirely persuaded that Miss Braithwaite had gone forever…yes, that must be it. Why had Papa said nothing to her of his feelings? Really, he was too shy and you couldn't blame poor Rosalind for thinking as she did. Cecily was so distracted by her misery that she almost bumped into her father, who was striding swiftly in the opposite direction.

"Cecily?" he said. "Where have you been? You look quite pale and there are shadows under your eyes. Are you ill?"

"Papa! I've been to see Rosalind. She's going abroad. She's packing."

Papa left Cecily where she was in the middle of the pavement and began to run toward the Templeton house. Cecily followed, as quickly as she could and was in time to see him disappear inside. The sun was shining brightly and she decided to wait for him. She imagined the terrible scene that would be going on in the parlor. Rosalind would tell Papa she was going abroad. Would he be broken-hearted? How Cecily wished she had a father whose feelings were easier to guess at! He would probably come out looking crestfallen and sad, and they'd go home together. She gathered her skirts about her and perched on the low wall with her back against the railings of the Templeton house. She was sure she wouldn't have long to wait.

Cecily was trying to write to Aunt Lizzie with Mossy lying curled up on her lap, which was rather difficult. Nevertheless, she had to tell the story of what happened after she'd said goodbye to Rosalind.

I sat on the wall, she wrote, *for such a long time. I didn't dare go and knock on the door at the Templetons' again, so I went to see Amy and tell her, and then we looked out of their front bedroom window for the rest of the afternoon. In the end, Papa and Rosalind came out together arm-in-arm and went off to the river. They are in love, Aunt Lizzie. Amy says so. They spend a great deal of time together, and Rosalind comes to Number Six almost every day. Amy says Papa is out of practice because he hasn't been in love for the six years since Mama died.*

Cecily put down her pen and fell to stroking Mossy's back. She wouldn't tell Aunt Lizzie, and she hadn't yet told Amy, that she'd looked out of the nursery window last night, at twilight, and seen Papa and Rosalind kissing under the walnut tree. She and Sam might have a new mama after all. If there was to be a wedding, she would redecorate the dollhouse in honor of the occasion. The *Willow* pattern wallpaper Rosalind had given her a few weeks ago lay in her chest of drawers and she would take it out and measure it for some of the main rooms. Cecily leaned her head on her hand and lost herself in happy daydreams, her letter unfinished on the table in front of her. Perhaps Rosalind would let her become a kind of apprentice and come to the studio sometimes where she worked. She would learn very quickly and soon she'd know enough to take every kind of photograph. "Ah yes, Miss Rosalind's young assistant," everyone would say. Cecily smiled to herself as she imagined the scene.

She moved her legs a little and startled Mossy, who jumped down and made for the door, with her tail held high.

"Goodbye, Mossy," Cecily said and then turned to write her letter again. *Can you keep a secret, Aunt Lizzie? Do not tell anyone, but I think Papa will soon ask Rosalind to marry him, and we will have a new mama…*

Cecily had a vision of herself in a bridesmaid's dress taking off a pretty hat trimmed with roses and ribbons and lace, in order to cover her head with the black cloth again, ready to look through the lens and compose the perfect image of her papa and his new bride. She sucked the end of her pen and wrote: *If there*

is to be a wedding, I might be allowed to take some of the
pictures, for a bride cannot photograph herself, can she?
I hope so much that Rosalind will let me take her place
behind the camera on that day…

Then she wished her aunt an affectionate farewell,
signed the letter with her name, and added a whole
row of kisses.

Glossary

nursery maid – a girl employed to assist in taking care of the children of a family, who would report to the nurse or nanny. Her duties would include tidying the nursery, supervising the children and seeing that they were dressed properly

morning room – a sitting room, used during daylight hours. Less formal than a drawing room

"lost a sixpence, found a farthing" – a farthing was worth much less than a sixpence (there were four farthings in one penny and six pennies in one sixpence, so one sixpence was worth twenty-four farthings), so this expression meant that someone looked unhappy

AUTHOR'S NOTE

I was very happy to be asked to join Linda Newbery and Ann Turnbull in telling the stories of the inhabitants of Number 6, Chelsea Walk. This book is a close companion to *Girls with Courage*, sharing not only a setting but also some of the same characters.

I love the 1890s. I like the art, the literature and especially the theater of those years and when I discovered that the first night of Oscar Wilde's *The Importance of Being Earnest* was on the 14th of February, I had a jumping-off point for my book.

I'm interested in photography. It's changed a lot since the 1890s. Everyone nowadays is fully equipped at all times with a camera in their smartphone. We take selfies, we photograph our lunch, we send pictures around the world on social media and think nothing of it. In the nineteenth century, things were vastly different but photography then was making enormous technological strides which led eventually to a time when everyone is a photographer.

I'm grateful to Angelo Hornak for guidance in technical matters and also to Laura Cecil for her help and advice.

It's been a pleasure to work with Linda and Ann and I'm grateful to Becky Walker for her help with this reissue. I'm really pleased that our books are reappearing in a lovely new format.

About the Author

Adèle Geras was born in Jerusalem and before the age of eleven had lived in Cyprus, Nigeria and North Borneo. She studied French and Spanish at Oxford University and taught French before becoming a full-time writer. She has written more than ninety books for children and young adults as well as six novels for adults.

She lives in Cambridge and has two daughters and four grandchildren.

To find out more about Adèle Geras, you can visit her website: www.adelegeras.com.

Usborne Quicklinks

For links to websites where you can find out more about photography and famous artists in Cecily's time and learn about everyday life at the end of the Victorian age, go to the Usborne Quicklinks website at www.usborne.com/quicklinks and type in the title of this book.

At Usborne Quicklinks you can:

- See examples of Victorian photographs and daguerreotypes
- Take a tour of a Victorian home
- Examine Pre-Raphaelite and Impressionist paintings and find out about the artists
- See some of the fashions of the day

Please follow the online safety guidelines at the Usborne Quicklinks website.

6 Chelsea Walk

1914

Girls
for the
Vote

LINDA NEWBERY

USBORNE

For Megan, of course

Contents

Basement

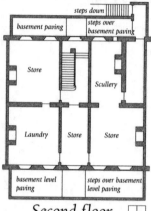

First-floor apartment

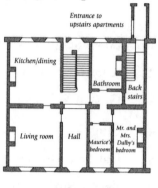

Second-floor apartment

Third-floor apartment

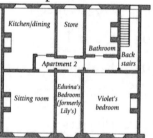

Roof space

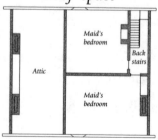

CHAPTER ONE

New Neighbors

The swing tree had always been Polly's favorite part of the garden. She came here to sit, or to read, or to watch the birds squabbling over thrown bread; or she came to swing. She liked to push herself as high as she could, her stretched-out feet pointing at Lily's bedroom on the third floor, till she almost felt she could launch herself from the swing seat and land neatly on the mat beside Lily's bed.

But now it wasn't Lily's bedroom, not anymore, and today Polly couldn't find the energy for proper swinging.

Until last week, she and Lily had come here together – to be by themselves, to talk and giggle and share secrets. Now there was no Lily, no one to share anything, and Polly didn't even want to look up at the top-floor apartment. For nearly a week, the windows had been blank and empty. Today the new people were moving in, and they were going to be duller than dull, she just knew it. It was so unfair!

Polly sat glumly, twisting the swing seat one way, then the other. She dragged her feet on the scuffed bare earth underneath.

She and Lily had been best friends for seven years, ever since Polly and her parents had moved into Number Six, Chelsea Walk. As their mothers were good friends too, Polly and Lily had shared a nanny and attended the same school; they had walked along the Thames Embankment and picnicked in Ranelagh

Gardens; they both had piano lessons with Lily's Aunt Dorothy, who lived nearby. Now Lily's mother was ill, and the family had moved to Tunbridge Wells, where the healthy air would do her good, Dr. Mayes said. All Lily's family's possessions and furniture had been carried out, less than a week ago.

This afternoon, Polly had arrived home from school to find a van parked outside, and boxes and crates being carried in by the very same men, three of them, in flat caps. What a strange job it must be, Polly thought – carting people's whole lives from one place to the next, swapping people around like books on shelves! She felt resentful of the newcomers. There hadn't been time to get used to Lily being gone, let alone to face the thought of new people moving in, putting their own pictures and ornaments where Lily's had been, making it all different.

"Lily can come to stay, sometimes," Polly's mother had said yesterday, seeing her gloomy face. "Tunbridge Wells isn't that far away. You haven't said goodbye to her forever and ever. And there's still Maurice!"

Maurice! Grownups simply didn't understand. As if Maurice could even begin to replace Lily! Polly glowered at the windows of the Dalbys' first-floor apartment. Polly's mother and Mrs. Dalby often had afternoon tea together or sat chatting while they sewed, but that didn't mean Polly was going to be friends with Horrid Maurice. He was the worst boy she knew. Since she didn't know many boys, this was less of an insult than she'd have liked; but she felt sure that even if she knew hundreds and hundreds, Maurice would still be the one she detested most.

If ever he saw Polly and Lily playing in the garden, he used to come out purely to pester them. He was twelve, the same as they were; but as Lily remarked loftily, "He's only a boy. They always seem younger than girls for their age." Once, he'd sneaked up behind Polly with a toad he'd found at the end of the garden, holding it so close that she came face to face with it when she turned around, and couldn't help shrieking with horror. That piercing shriek – she hadn't known she could make such a sound – had annoyed her as much as it had amused Maurice; she never usually made a fuss about mice, spiders or other crawly creatures. Another time, he had thrown Eugenie, Lily's doll, high into the branches of the walnut tree, where her long hair had become so firmly snagged on twigs that Polly had to call the gardener to bring a ladder and climb to the rescue.

Why couldn't it have been *Maurice's* mother who was ill and needed the Tunbridge Wells air?

And now a new disappointment! The one hope remaining to Polly was that the new occupants of Apartment Three would have a daughter her own age – not, of course, one she would like as much as Lily, because that would be disloyal, but still someone who could fill the friend gap. But Papa had heard that the new people weren't a family at all, but a pair of spinsters: Miss Cross and Miss Rutherford. Polly wrinkled her nose when she heard the names. She imagined the Misses Cross and Rutherford as elderly ladies, dressed stiffly in black and purple and old lace that smelled of mothballs. Miss Cross would be cross, of course – probably they both would. They'd look down long noses at her and would sniff in disapproval if she played in the garden. They'd be hard of hearing and would cup their hands to their ears if she tried to speak to them, so that she'd have to repeat everything three times. They might even be so deaf as to use ear trumpets. Yet their ears would be sharply tuned to any noise she made on the back stairs or in her bedroom; there would be complaints to Mama and Papa. She knew it! She disliked them already.

"Oh, but this is lovely!" said a voice, close behind her.

Polly turned. Two people had come out of the doorway that led to the back stairs: both young women, dressed alike in navy-blue skirts and white blouses. The taller and thinner of the two was looking this way and that, giving excited little claps of her hands;

the other, dark-haired, stocky and hatless, gazed around her as she came down the steps to the grass.

"We could hardly have done better!" the tall one went on. "And look, this tree – lovely shade on a hot day – oh! Hello! I'm so sorry if we startled you."

They were coming toward her, smiling and interested, as if a girl on a swing were the most exciting thing they could hope to find in a garden. Polly felt annoyed with herself; she could have dodged out of sight behind the blackcurrant bushes, to look and listen without being seen.

Slowly, she got up from the swing seat, and tugged at her skirt. "Only for a moment." She looked from one face to the other. These two must be nieces, or something, of the old ladies who were moving in; spinsters, of course, wouldn't have daughters or granddaughters.

"You live here, do you?" the shorter one asked.

"Yes. Up there, in the middle apartment." Polly pointed to the second-floor windows.

"Then we're going to be neighbors!" exclaimed the

tall young woman, who seemed ready to be delighted by everything. "How marvelous! We must introduce ourselves properly. How do you do? I'm Edwina Rutherford, and this is Violet Cross." She held out a hand to shake Polly's. "Do tell us who you are!"

"Oh!" Polly was unable to hide her surprise. "But you're not – I mean, I thought – I thought you'd be cross and old!" It came out, just like that, before she could stop herself; she blushed at her rudeness.

Miss Rutherford laughed, not seeming to mind. "I *feel* old, sometimes. *Look* old, sometimes." And Polly noticed that her face, under her hat brim, looked pale and drawn, like that of a very ill person who was venturing out for the first time after weeks on a sickbed. "As for Violet –" Miss Rutherford turned to her friend – "Cross by name, kindly by nature!"

"And your name?" prompted Miss Cross.

"Polly. Paulina Elizabeth Genevieve Stubbs, but I'm always called Polly. So you're really the people moving in upstairs?"

Miss Rutherford laughed. "We really are. We've come outside to give ourselves a rest from boxes and dust and decisions. Maybe you could show us around the garden?"

Polly wasn't sure what to show them that they couldn't see easily for themselves, but she said, "Yes, of course." Miss Rutherford made a big show of setting off on a Grand Tour, adjusting her hat, looking around expectantly, and putting her best foot forward.

"Now, Edwina," said Miss Cross, glancing anxiously at her, "you're not to go over-tiring yourself. It's been a long day. You ought to be putting your feet up. The doctor said—"

"I can rest later," Miss Rutherford assured her. But she took the offered arm, and leaned slightly against her friend as they took a few steps down the garden. Only a few steps, because Polly wanted them to have a proper look at the tree. She stood back to gaze up at it, its cracked bark and the spreading canopy of leaves, and the branch that had the swing's ropes lashed round it.

"We'll start here. This tree," she said proudly, "is a walnut tree. We get walnuts from it in autumn. The Romans, you know, brought walnuts when they came to England, and planted them. This one was grown from a walnut by a girl who lived here years and years ago. And now it's big enough to swing from!"

"How marvelous!" Miss Rutherford tilted back her head to look at the upper branches. "And how do you know that?"

"Mrs. Parks told me. She's our cook."

"Imagine!" said Miss Rutherford. "One little walnut, growing into a tree this size! I shall find a nut in autumn and try to grow a new tree myself. There," she added, looking sidelong at Miss Cross, "you see what great things can grow from small beginnings! What an inspiration, to look out of our window and see this every day!"

"You got more than enough inspiration if you

ask me," said Miss Cross, almost crossly.

Polly looked at them with interest. She had thought at first that they might be cousins, but now decided that they couldn't be related at all; they looked so unalike, and their voices were very different, too. Whereas Miss Rutherford spoke in the clear, confident tone of most people who lived in this part of Chelsea, Miss Cross's way of speaking was less refined – the way a servant might speak. Polly liked her friendly directness, but her accent was what Mama called common. Polly wondered if maybe she was looking after Miss Rutherford – perhaps she was a paid nurse, or companion. Miss Rutherford had the liveliest blue eyes, that seemed to dart around taking in everything; but she also looked as tired as a candle on its last sputter. Her skin looked almost transparent, there were shadows under her eyes, and she was so thin that – as Mama would say – a puff of wind would blow her over. And Miss Cross had mentioned the doctor, and resting. Mama saw the doctor quite often, and was supposed to rest each afternoon with her feet up on the couch, but that was because of the new baby that was on the way. That couldn't possibly be the cause of Miss Rutherford's frailness.

"Excuse me, Miss Rutherford –" Polly ventured.

"Oh, please – call me Edwina, and Violet, Violet! Miss Rutherford makes me feel like an elderly spinster! You don't want us to call you Miss Stubbs, do you? May we call you Polly?"

"Yes, of course. Well, er – Edwina," Polly continued awkwardly, not used to calling grownups by their first names, "I hope you won't think I'm rude, but are you ill?"

"Well, like –" Miss Cross, Violet, began, but Edwina cut her short, fixing Polly with her straight blue gaze.

"Yes, Polly, in a way I have been ill. You see, I've just been released from prison."

CHAPTER TWO

A Letter to Lily

...Sports Day, and an outing to Kew, but it isn't nearly as much fun without you, Polly wrote, forming the letters carefully. *Whenever we have partners I have to go with Maudie Marchant, just because no one else wants to. I call her Moody Marchant.*

She was at the dining table, supposedly doing her French homework. The writing paper – smooth cream bond, with *Flat 2, 6 Chelsea Walk* printed in curling script – rested on the pages of her French book, so that it could be hidden if Mama came unexpectedly into the room. As Mrs. Dalby was here, and she and Mama were having tea in the drawing room, Polly knew she was safe as long as she could hear the two alternating voices; if the conversation stopped and footsteps came this way, there would be time to hide the letter and pretend to be concentrating very hard on French conjugations.

But something very exciting has happened, Polly wrote on, *and it's to do with the new people in your apartment!* She hesitated – would this make Lily feel she had been too easily replaced? She thought, gazed at the piano, and wrote again. *It won't be the same as having you here, but they are not the two prim old ladies I expected. Their names are Edwina Rutherford and Violet Cross, and they want to be friends. I don't mean friends like you and me, they are too old for that, but friendly, anyway. They have already told me all sorts of things! It is hard to tell how old they are – grownup, but not very. Anyway, they are much younger than my mama or yours. And, you'll never guess –*

Miss McFarlane at school said that a sentence should never begin with *and*, but sometimes it seemed just right. Polly stopped writing again and leaned her chin on her hand, looking out into the branches of the walnut tree. At this height, on the second floor, it filled the window with green. Amazing, the way it branched and branched, so that from up here Polly had a squirrel's-eye view, looking through the mass of leaves, each one divided into seven leaflets, with the dangling, catkin-like flowers that made the whole tree seem decorated for summer. Papa had talked about getting it cut down, complaining that it was too tall for the garden and too close to the house and that it blocked the light, but Polly and Mama had argued passionately that it must stay. Most houses had gardens, but not every house had its own walnut tree! And Papa enjoyed eating the walnuts at

Christmas, and having them pickled for the rest of the year. Mrs. Parks, the cook-housekeeper, had her own special way of pickling, which Papa said was better than anyone else's.

Polly's mind flicked back to the thrilling moment when Edwina announced that she'd been in prison. Prison! Polly had felt her mouth opening in a fish-like gape. Only very bad people went to prison, didn't they? Edwina looked and sounded so ladylike that Polly couldn't begin to imagine what crime she might have committed.

Violet had laughed. "You ought to be more careful about coming straight out with things," she told her friend. "Look how you've shocked Polly now! Don't worry," she told Polly, "she's not a thief or a murderer!"

"No, I didn't think –" Polly faltered, unsure what she *did* think. "But, then, what did you –?"

"I was sent to Holloway Prison for attacking a policeman outside Buckingham Palace." For a moment, Edwina looked even taller, and her eyes fierier.

"Attacking – oh! You're a –" Newspaper headlines flashed into Polly's head; she thought of her father reading *The Times* at breakfast, shaking his head at what the world was coming to. "You're one of those suffragettes!"

Edwina nodded. "I am. And very proud of it."

According to Papa, it was completely disgraceful; ladies getting up to such antics, as he called them. How exciting, though, Polly thought: How brave, to shout in the streets and confront the police and not be told what to do! How marvelous to be so *unladylike*! Being ladylike all the time must be very, very dull.

"Are you one, too?" she asked Violet. "A suffragette?"

She noticed the quick glance that passed between the two young women: the faintest suggestion of a smile from Edwina, a tightening of the lips and tilt of the head from Violet. Then Violet answered:

"I'm a campaigner for votes for women, yes. Votes for everyone. I prefer suffragist to suffragette. Let's just say, Edwina and me don't always see eye to eye on getting our points made. I don't go round thumping policemen, for a start, nor throwing myself under racehorses, neither. Edwina, she'd do it soon as cross the road."

"You didn't –?"

"Of course not," Edwina said, smiling. Then her face became serious. "Violet was referring to Emily Davison, our brave comrade who sacrificed herself to the Cause last summer."

Polly remembered that – the news vendors shouting in the streets, the front-page headlines. Emily Davison – Polly had forgotten the name – had gone to the Derby race meeting, and waited by the side of the track for the horses' thundering approach; then she had run out into the path of the King's own horse.

Now, at the table, Polly sat screwing and unscrewing the top of her pen, thinking about it, imagining herself as Emily Davison. What must she have been feeling? Merging with the crowd, feigning an interest in the race itself and which horse was likely to win – and all the time steeling herself for the moment of breaking free, ducking under the rails for that wild dash under the horses' flailing limbs. She had been killed – not immediately, but had been kicked and trampled so badly that she died in the hospital a few days later. Was that what she intended? And, having died, she would never know if women *did* get the vote, or whether they had to go on and on chaining themselves to railings, smashing windows, slashing paintings in galleries…

"Was it awful in prison?" Polly had asked Edwina, looking at her with a renewed shyness. It felt almost like talking to someone who had died, and come back to tell her about it.

Violet answered first. "Needn't have been as awful as Edwina made it. She refused to eat. Went on a hunger strike. You'll have read about it in the papers, I 'spect. She's done all that before, course. Nearly starved herself to death, she did, till they stuck a feeding tube down her neck." She darted a look at her friend. "Now the government's got a new way of dealing with it," she told Polly. "P'raps you know. No more force-feeding – no, they let the women starve themselves till they're fit to collapse. Then they let them out, but only till they've got enough strength to be arrested again."

"So you might have to go back to prison?" Polly said, in a small voice. Part of her mind was working on a new problem: *What will Mama and Papa say?*

"Not only might, but *will*," Edwina said, with what Polly already recognized as her stubborn look. "Cat and Mouse, it's called. You've seen the way a cat plays with a mouse, like a toy – letting it run, then clawing it back again? That's what the prison authorities are doing to us – playing with us, treating us as their victims! But one thing I can tell you, Polly, is – we will never give up the fight, never! Not till women have the same rights as men!"

Polly didn't think she had ever met anyone as determined as Edwina. Ill as she was, she seemed to burn with passion, her whole body trembling with it.

"Come on in now." Violet tugged at her friend's arm. "You're over-tired. You won't mind showing us the garden another time, will you, Polly? Time's getting on, there's still a lot to do."

"Please don't fuss! I'm perfectly well!" Edwina retorted. But she seemed to sag and become smaller, as if the last blaze of energy had been snuffed out. "All right, then. Just a little rest, before we unpack the books. Polly, I'm so glad we've made friends!" she added, finding the energy for a cheery wave. "You must come up and visit us when we're shipshape!"

Polly watched them go back across the grass and in at the side door that led to the upstairs apartments, Violet helping Edwina, who lifted her skirt with one hand and placed her feet very carefully on the step, like a doddery old lady. Inside, there were two staircases to be climbed to the top apartment. Lily and Polly used to bound up two at a time when no one was around to tell them off, but it would be a long climb for someone as weak as Edwina.

New friends! Had she really made new friends? How amazing that people so much older, and with such important things to do, should take notice of *her*!

She unscrewed her pen, and wrote: *They are suffragettes! They don't seem to agree on how to go about it, but one of them, Edwina, has actually been in prison and been on hunger strike, and –*

"Polly?"

Mama's voice in the hallway. Quickly, Polly slipped the letter between the pages of her French book and pretended to be aroused from deep thought.

"Yes, Mama?"

"You must be nearly finished, surely? Do come and join us."

Polly closed her books and went through to the drawing room, ushered by her mother. Mrs. Dalby, Maurice's mother, was sitting in a chair and half-turned toward the window; the tea tray was on a low table in front of her, and one of Mrs. Parks' special strawberry sponge cakes, sprinkled with powdered sugar.

"Hello, Polly. You're such a good girl, doing your homework so diligently!" said Mrs. Dalby, in the cooing voice Polly found so irritating. "Now do tell me." She sat forward, hands on her knees. "Maurice told me he saw you talking to our new neighbors, a little while ago! I'm just eaten up with curiosity – do tell me everything you've found out!"

CHAPTER THREE

Gossip

"Oh, not much, really," Polly said cautiously. Trust nosy old Maurice to have been watching! Not that there was anything wrong with talking in the garden, was there?

Mama, passing Polly a slice of cake, gave her a sidelong look. "You've spoken to them? Why ever didn't you tell me, when you came indoors?"

"Two young ladies, Maurice said. Are they sisters?" probed Mrs. Dalby.

"No, not sisters. Their names are Edwina Rutherford and Violet Cross."

"And where have they come from?"

Polly flicked a glance at Mrs. Dalby, then at her mother, tempted to say, "From Holloway Prison." Straightening the smile that twitched at her mouth, she replied instead, "I don't know. We only talked for a few moments, and it was mainly about – about the walnut tree."

"Didn't you find out anything about them at all?" said Mrs. Dalby, looking quite crestfallen. "Are they young women of private means? Presumably their families are renting the apartment for them? I shouldn't imagine they'd be working girls, would you, Catherine?" she asked Polly's mother. "There's a maid, my Elsie told me – living in one of the attic rooms."

"I shall invite them to tea!" declared Mama. "Then we'll meet them properly – find out all about them. Early next week, I shall suggest – when they've had time to settle themselves. You must come as well, Meredith!"

Polly felt uneasy. She wanted to keep her new friends to herself.

"I'd be delighted," said Mrs. Dalby. "After all, we ought to know who's living under our roof. But I really must be going." She got to her feet, straightened her skirt and adjusted the lace collar of her blouse. "Polly, do come down and play chess with Maurice if you get lonely – I know how badly you must be missing Lily. Now, Catherine, my dear, make sure you look after yourself." She patted Mama's arm. "Not too much standing, remember! I'm sure I've told you, when I was expecting Maurice, how dreadfully my ankles swelled? Rest every afternoon with my feet up, that's what the doctor advised, but of course I'm far too active for that. You must be so excited, Polly! Not much longer to wait. Such fun it'll be, having a little brother."

Polly swallowed a mouthful of cake. "How do you know it'll be a brother?"

"Well, or sister. But –" Mrs. Dalby touched Mama's arm again, and gave her a twinkling look. "But I have a feeling it's a boy this time, and my feelings rarely let me down! Goodbye, then. Goodbye, dear." And at last she was gone, in a waft of lily-of-the-valley.

Mama rang the bell for Mrs. Parks to come for the tea things. She stood up in the awkward way she had developed since becoming so large; she stifled a yawn, and put a hand to the small of her back. "I really do think I'd better lie down and rest before dinner. Do make sure you put your things away, won't you, darling? You know how Papa hates to see things lying around. Did you finish your schoolwork?"

"Nearly," said Polly. "Mama, do *you* hope the new baby's going to be a boy?"

Mama looked at her. "Well, of course it would be lovely to have one of each! And Papa would be thrilled to have a son. But we shall both be delighted, whichever it is."

"Wasn't Papa thrilled when I was born? Was he disappointed?"

"Polly!" Mama touched Polly's hair, smoothing back a wayward strand that escaped from its pigtail. "No one was disappointed, of course not – you know we couldn't love you more, both of us! But you have to understand that there's a special thing about fathers and sons. A son, you see, will keep our name, and will marry and have children and grandchildren. Whereas you'll change your name when you get married, just as I did, and your children will have your husband's name, not Stubbs."

"Supposing I don't meet someone I want to marry?"

Mama laughed, and patted her shoulder. "Darling, of course you will! When you're old enough, you'll meet all sorts of suitable young men. Some young man will come along, don't you worry, who will think himself very lucky indeed! If you tidy up your things, there'll be time for your piano practice – there's a good girl. Dinner will be at six."

Polly went back to the dining table, her letter and her French homework, still thinking about her shadowy future husband. Mama hadn't really answered her question. Polly hadn't asked whether anyone would want to marry her; she had been wondering whether she would meet someone she might *choose*. It wasn't the same thing. Anyway, Polly wanted to be an explorer. She wanted to travel the world and see all sorts of places and people. There wouldn't be time for a husband, unless he was an explorer as well.

She couldn't imagine Edwina Rutherford waiting for some nice, suitable young man to come along and think himself very lucky. Nor Violet Cross.

Supposing the only suitable young man she met turned out to be Maurice? She'd sooner marry a duck-billed platypus, she thought, opening her French book at the page where the letter was hidden; she'd sooner marry a warthog. Lily, who had recently been to her cousin's wedding, had told Polly that in the marriage service, the bride had to promise to obey her husband. That meant doing whatever he told you, the way Mama always did what Papa said. Really, you might as well stay on at school, if someone was going to carry on telling you what to do and not do.

Imagine promising that to someone as slimy as Maurice! Polly unscrewed her pen lid and stuck out her tongue, making the sort of face Mrs. Parks said she should avoid, in case the wind changed and she got stuck like it. She'd rather marry a *toad*.

CHAPTER FOUR

Slug

"Can you imagine," Polly said to Maudie Marchant at morning break, "wanting something so badly that you'd die for it?"

Maudie finished chomping a mouthful of apple before answering. "No," she said at last. "If you were dead, what would be the point?"

"You might want something for someone else," Polly explained, "not just for yourself."

Maudie considered this possibility, nibbling around the apple core till it was little more than an extension of its stalk. "No. I can't think of anything I'd want *that* much. Can you?"

If Polly were honest, the answer would have been no; but instead she asked, "What about the suffragettes – you know, getting sent to prison and going on hunger strikes?"

"Oh, *them*." Maudie had eaten all there was to eat of the apple, but instead of flicking the core into the bushes at the edge of the playground, as Polly would have done, she held it carefully by the stalk, no doubt waiting to put it in the litter bin on the way back to the classroom: Maudie did everything according to the rules. "My father says they're just vandals and hooligans. Lock them up and throw away the key, that's what he says. Have them horsewhipped. If they behave like gangs of ruffians, making trouble in the streets, how do they *expect* to get the vote?"

Polly was silent for a moment. Her father said

exactly the same sort of thing, tisking as he read the newspaper, reading out bits to Mama. He seemed to think that the campaigning women belonged to an entirely different species from his wife, who sat demurely with her needlework, nodding and agreeing with whatever he said. What was Papa going to say when he found out that two suffragettes (or one suffragette and one suffragist: Polly was unclear about the distinction) were living in the very same house, sharing his roof? What would he say about Mama inviting them to tea? Perhaps, Polly thought, she ought to warn them; tell them to keep quiet, and talk only about the weather and the latest fashions and other polite, everyday things. Or perhaps it would be better if they didn't come at all, if they just smiled politely and said *How do you do?* to anyone they met on the way in or out.

In the classroom, Polly paused by the globe on the window table to play her favorite game. She made it spin on its stem as fast as it would go; then she closed her eyes, touched a finger to the whirling surface – but not hard enough to slow its turning – and waited for it to come to a complete stop. Then she looked at where her finger was resting, and thought: *That's where I might go, one day, when I can go anywhere I like.* It felt a bit like someone telling her fortune by reading a crystal ball, only this ball had all the countries of the world printed on it. Yesterday it had been Alaska, and she'd imagined snowy wastes, frozen rivers, and gold-panners. Today – she looked carefully – her finger was planted in the middle of the Pacific Ocean, nowhere near any land at all. Of course, explorers would have to spend months at a time on sea voyages. She might be seasick, but she would have to put up with that…

"Did I lend you my new pen-wiper?" Maudie asked. Polly sighed with impatience, pulled back to the schoolroom, and the prospect of algebra with Miss Dawes.

Lily's departure had taken all the fun out of dawdling home and finding detours, going to see the dairy horses in Old Church Street, or up to the King's Road to look in shop windows, or the long way back along the Embankment to watch the boats going past and sniff the salty air that carried a tang of the sea.

Back at home, Polly took her bookbag upstairs, then went straight out to the swing tree in the hope of seeing the new neighbors there. Or maybe they would see her, and come out to finish their "tour"?

But Maurice was there instead, sitting on the swing – *her* swing! – scuffing his feet on the bare earth underneath, and grinning at her. He was in the brown uniform of his school, St. Dunstan's. St. *Dung*stan's, Polly called it, as the boys' blazers were exactly the color of the heaped, steaming manure left in the road by tradesmen's horses.

"Greetings, Pegs." His grin widened. His red hair was like a thatch, and his face all freckled. *Pegs* was his nickname for her, since he'd seen her initials on her pencil box. She hated being called that. It made her think of clothes pegs, peg legs, square pegs in round holes.

"Hello, Horrible Horace."

Maurice smiled back as if she'd said something nice. It was impossible to offend him.

"Did you know there's a rhyme about walnut trees?" he said, reaching out to touch its bark. "It goes like this: *A dog, a wife and a walnut tree, the more you beat them, the better they be.* My grandad told me."

"That's stupid," Polly retorted. "It's cruel to beat people *or* dogs. And why would anyone beat a walnut tree? And why would anyone be better for being beaten? It would only make you bad-tempered and upset."

Maurice grinned again, as if he knew something she didn't. Lazily, he got off the swing. "Come and see what I've found."

She might have guessed it would be something unpleasant. At the farthest end of the garden, where the shrubs grew thickly, he pushed aside the lowest leaves of a hydrangea, and revealed an enormous slug – black and shiny, big as a sausage – in the dampness underneath.

"Urrgh!" Polly couldn't help leaping back. There, he'd made her do it again! – behave just as he wanted. She wasn't usually silly about slugs or other creeping forms of life. After all, she was going to meet all kinds of creatures – slimy or scaly, feathered or furred – when she became an explorer. She'd be very annoyed with herself if she jumped back squealing each time she came across something strange.

"Do you know what it is?" Maurice asked.

"Of course I do. It's a slug, silly. One of your relations, I expect. Tell the gardener to get rid of it."

"It's not just an *ordinary* slug." Maurice made his eyes round and his voice low and menacing. "It's the very rare Nocturnal Man-Eating Slug, feared by all travelers and explorers. Do you know what they do? They wait till nighttime, then they creep across the lawn. They get into houses, creep in through cellar openings and ventilation grilles. There's no way of keeping them out. Then they smell out their victims. They like flesh – that's why they're so enormous. Specially children's flesh – it's not so tough. While you're fast asleep, they come sliming all over you, waiting to feast on flesh—"

"Oh, stop it!" Polly felt the skin on her arms and legs creeping, and only by an effort of will forced herself not to turn and run. "They'll find *you* first then, won't they, on the first floor? I'd watch out if I were you." She turned to claim the swing. "And be very careful not to sleep with your mouth open," she added over her shoulder.

Reaching the swing, she heard the creak of a window opening above her, and a voice called down. "Polly!"

She stepped back to see past the tree branches and up to the third floor, where Violet Cross was shaking a duster out of the window. "I've got the kettle on," Violet called. "Want to come and see the chaos up here?"

Maurice hadn't followed, and was poking about in the undergrowth, no doubt looking for more man-eating slugs, but she made a point of calling back to him, "Excuse me. I've got someone *interesting* to talk to."

CHAPTER FIVE

Cat and Mouse

It was only after Polly had been in the drawing room of the top floor for ten minutes that she remembered to feel sad that it was no longer Lily's home. It hardly looked the same at all: the familiar furniture had gone, there were new curtains up at the window, and the floor was stacked with boxes, higgledy-piggledy.

"Excuse the mess," Edwina said, indicating the boxes. "We've got so many books, and nowhere to put them, till we get extra shelves put up. But do sit on my new chaise longue. Don't you think it's just beautiful?" She gestured toward the seat that seemed to take pride of place, upholstered in green velvet and with a scrolled back and armrest.

"As if we haven't got enough bits and pieces, she has to go buying more!" Violet said, rolling her eyes upward.

"It was in the window of Hauptmann's, in the King's Road. I just couldn't resist treating myself to it," Edwina explained. "I've always wanted one, and thought I deserved a coming-out-of-prison present. You can test it for comfort, Polly."

Polly settled herself on the chaise longue while Edwina perched on a crate and Violet settled on the windowsill to wait for the tea to brew. It was all so different from Polly's mother's way of inviting people to tea. Mama would never dream of shouting to someone from a window, nor of inviting them in on the spur of the moment. Invitations to tea were always made in advance, and Mrs. Parks would bake a cake and prepare bread and butter, or thin sandwiches with the crusts cut off.

And Mama would never contemplate letting anyone through the door if the apartment was untidy – not that it ever was, with Mrs. Parks in charge. Here the tea was in mugs, and biscuits were eaten straight from the tin. Besides Violet and Edwina, there was a pretty, pert-faced girl of about eighteen, introduced as "Kitty, who looks after us," and who must be the maid, but it was Violet who poured the tea and handed it around.

"Just imagine!" cried Edwina, who seemed full of energy this afternoon, not tired at all. "This whole house once belonged to one family! Your apartment, Polly, *and* the one on the first floor, *and* this one, *and* the servants' bedrooms in the attic – how splendidly people used to live!"

"*Some* people," Violet corrected.

"Well, of course that's what I meant."

"If you go into the Dalbys' apartment, on the first

floor, you can see how it used to be," Polly said, finding herself less shy than she had expected; the others listened to her, smiling and attentive, just as if she were someone their own age. "That's the one my mother would really like to live in. It's got black and white marble tiles in the hall and an archway that leads to the stairs – and then the big wide staircase that doesn't lead anywhere! It goes halfway up, turns the corner, then heads straight for a wall – the wall and the extra bit of floor that were put in when the house was split into separate apartments. But you can see what a grand house it used to be, when you could walk straight on up. Then, it was only the servants that used our back stairs. Mrs. Parks told me."

"I'd love to have seen it!" said Edwina.

She could easily have been the lady of the house, Polly thought. Her fair hair was swept back from her face and pinned up neatly; with her straight nose and sharp chin she looked as well-bred as a greyhound or a racehorse; her clothes – a dark skirt, and high-

collared cream blouse with embroidered panels –
looked expensive and well made. She had the sort of
voice that could easily be used for ordering servants
about, or for complaining that the knives and forks
weren't polished highly enough. Violet, with her
blouse coming untucked from her skirt, and the toes
of her shoes scuffed, looked more like the person who
did the polishing, or took the orders. Polly still hadn't
decided whether Violet, as well as Kitty, worked for
Edwina in some way. It was hard to tell in such a
strange set-up. None of the other grownups Polly
knew would have dreamed of introducing the maid,
just as if she were their equal.

"Lend a hand folding pamphlets, Poll?" Violet,
having handed around the sugar bowl and the one
spoon that could be found, and taken one of the mugs
to Kitty in the kitchen, now carried yet another box
into the room. "We're holding a meeting here tonight,
and I've only just picked these up from the printer's
on my way home from work."

"Work?" Polly echoed, remembering Mrs. Dalby's questions.

Violet glanced at her. "That's right. I work in the WSPU office. Women's Social and Political Union. Typewriting, filing, bit of accounting. I love it!"

Real work, Polly thought – just like Papa, who went off to the bank every morning and did important things there. What would Mrs. Dalby make of that? Polly wondered. Ladies didn't work, so that must mean Violet wasn't a lady, whereas Edwina clearly was. But Violet sounded as if she'd *choose* to work, even if she didn't have to.

"We'll be needing these for the meeting." Edwina ripped open the box. "We're planning a march to the Town Hall, in two weeks. The Lord Mayor and the councilors are holding a special evening reception there, and a banquet. It's going to turn out much more exciting than they think!"

"So you'll both be marching?" Polly asked, remembering yesterday's difference of opinion.

"Well, yes – but Edwina's plan is to get re-arrested and taken back to Holloway," said Violet, stacking sheets of paper in piles. "That's if she manages to stay out of prison till then," she added, with one of the meaningful looks at her friend that Polly took as a sign that they'd argued about this.

"Why? What are you going to do?" Polly imagined Edwina throwing bricks at the Town Hall windows, or attacking the Lord Mayor himself, flying at him like a wildcat as he mounted the steps, resplendent in his robe and chains.

"I won't have to do anything. Just be there. Cat and Mouse, remember," Edwina said, making her hands like claws. "But actually I shall be making a speech."

"She's still officially in Holloway," Violet said, with a wry shake of her head. "Only let out to get her strength back. Soon as the Cats see she's fit enough to go speechifying and waving banners in the King's Road, she'll be locked up again."

"So why go, then?" Polly appealed to Edwina. "Couldn't you just stay here, out of sight? After all, mice don't usually march about in front of cats – they run away behind the baseboards!"

Violet shook her head. "Wouldn't suit Edwina, being *that* mouse-like. Bit too much tiger about her, if you ask me."

"What would be the point of hiding?" Edwina asked Polly, with one of her steely looks.

"Well!" It seemed so obvious. "So you don't have to go back and be ill again. Just when you're starting to get better."

"Oh, Polly." Violet shook her head. "Edwina *wants* to go back to Holloway. Go on a hunger strike again. Die, if need be. It's good publicity, see, for the Cause."

"You don't really want to die, do you?" Polly asked Edwina, in a small, shocked voice.

Edwina laughed. "Not till I've had the chance to vote! No, I know my own strengths and weaknesses well enough. What I've done is nothing, compared to Emmeline and Sylvia. I've only been arrested three times and sentenced twice. Sylvia's been in and out of prison for the last eight years!"

"Didn't realize it was a competition," Violet said lightly. "And where's your other heroine – Christabel? Run away to Paris, sending instructions to the rest of us, saying what we're to do next! Here, Polly. Fold them twice, like this, so they'll fit the envelopes. You fold, I'll stick them in, Edwina can write the addresses."

The people they were talking about – Emmeline, Sylvia and Christabel – were, Polly knew, the famous Mrs. Pankhurst and her daughters. This was so exciting, she thought – hearing Violet and Edwina talk about people who appeared in the newspapers, and who everyone had heard of! She must tell Lily in her next letter. Edwina cleared a space on a cluttered table and found a pen, while Polly looked at the folded leaflet Violet had given her.

THE CAT AND MOUSE ACT
MUST NOT DETER US FROM
MAKING OUR VIEWS KNOWN!

JOIN THE **WSPU** PROTEST MARCH
TO THE CHELSEA TOWN HALL TO
CONFRONT THE LORD MAYOR
AND COUNCILORS

AT AN IMPORTANT
CIVIC RECEPTION AND BANQUET.

ASSEMBLE AT SPEAKER'S CORNER,
HYDE PARK,
5pm, SATURDAY 11th JULY.

BRING BANNERS,
WEAR **WSPU** COLORS.

**WOMEN'S SOCIAL
&
POLITICAL UNION**

Immediately, Polly wanted to go too, but she couldn't help remarking, "Not all women want the vote, though, do they? Mama, and Mrs. Dalby, and Great Aunt Millicent – *they* don't. I've heard them talking about it."

"What do they say?" said Edwina, with her head down, writing.

Polly tried to remember. "Things like – *Leave it to the men. No need for us to trouble our heads*. That sort of thing."

Edwina looked up, amused; she made a snorting noise, just like the milkman's horse. "*Leave it to the men?* Yes, and see where that's got us! Strikes, the Irish Question, dreadful conditions in factories, desperate poverty in the East End – that's how good the politicians are at sorting things out!"

Polly didn't know much about any of these things. "I'm only saying what –"

"Yes, I know – but what your aunt and mother say, that's a way of not having to think for themselves!

Shouldn't women have a say in who represents us in Parliament? Shouldn't we be entitled to put our views?"

"All right, Edie, you're not on your soapbox now," Violet said calmly. "No need to start yelling. Polly can hear you all right."

Edwina stopped in mid-breath, and smiled apologetically at Polly. "Sorry. Sorry. I get carried away. But it's quite true, you know! When you grow up, Polly, unless the government sees sense, you won't be entitled to vote, won't have a say in the running of the country – no matter how sensible, how accomplished, how capable or thoughtful you are. Whereas – think of the most thuggish, nasty boy you know –"

"Maurice," Polly said, without hesitation.

"Maurice? All right – or, say, someone who grows up to be a drunkard, who gambles away his money, who beats his wife and ill-treats his children – *he'll* be entitled to vote, but you won't. Does that seem fair to you?"

"No!" said Polly hotly. "Of course it isn't!"

Violet licked and sealed an envelope. "She won't stop till you're a signed-up member of the WSPU, Polly, you realize that?"

"Well, it's important!" Edwina said. "We need a new generation of women to come along and take over when we've exhausted ourselves –"

"– when you've starved yourself to death, you mean. Have another cookie."

"The thing is, Polly, you can make up your own mind." Edwina took a chocolate cream with one hand and reached for an envelope with the other. "You don't have to let anyone else tell you what to think. Not even me."

Polly was struck by a new thought. "Our new baby – my baby brother, assuming he's a boy, which everyone seems to think – when he grows up, he'll be able to vote, even though he's not even born yet, and I won't, even though I'm older!" She looked from Edwina's face to Violet's. "That's *definitely* not right, is it?"

"No, it's not," said Violet.

Edwina smiled at her. "There, you see – you're thinking for yourself. Seeing how things are. Wondering if things ought to change. Are you any good at sewing, Polly?"

"Sewing?" Polly echoed. Sewing was exactly the sort of thing Mama approved of – a long way from protesting in the streets!

"Banners." Edwina nodded toward a bulging package under the table. "All that fabric's got to be turned into banners. Purple, white and green, with lettering. Will you help us?"

Polly wasn't much good at sewing – "all fingers and thumbs" Miss Thripp called her at school; Lily was the one who was neat and deft with a needle. But she answered without hesitation. "Yes. Yes, of course I will."

CHAPTER SIX

Secret Suffragette

In the early hours of Monday morning, Polly lay in bed, hot, restless and worrying.

She *had* been asleep, but now, at half past two in the morning (she had crept out to the hall, to check by the grandfather clock) she felt wider awake than ever. With the new electric lights, she could easily have turned on her lamp to read, but felt certain she wouldn't be able to concentrate. She had pushed back the sheets, blanket and quilt, but still felt hot and fidgety.

She was hungry, too, and that wasn't a very good beginning to the day, as she had decided not to eat anything at all for twenty-four hours. If Edwina could go without food for nearly a week, Polly wanted to prove to herself that she could manage just one day. Now that she was a suffragette, or suffragist, she would have to be willing to put herself to the test. She hadn't told anyone she was a suffragette; but how could she not be, now that it had been explained to her? It was so obviously unreasonable for things to continue as they were. If she felt herself wavering, Polly had only to think of Maurice, and his smug, superior smile. Why should he think himself more important than her, just because he happened to be a boy?

What was keeping her awake was the problem of what Mama would say when she found out that Violet and Edwina were suffragettes, as she must surely discover when Edwina came to tea tomorrow – no, to*day*. It would have to be Edwina on her own, since Violet would be at work. Suffragettes, to Mama, were a strange new breed of savage women, with their weapons and their firebombs, their angry voices and their fierce determination.

"What must their husbands think?" Polly had heard her remark to Meredith Dalby. "Their families? How can they bear to demean themselves by shouting in the streets?"

Polly couldn't imagine Mama shouting in the street, not even if there were a burglary, or a fire! To Mama, *decorum* was the rule for female behavior. "A little more decorum, please, girls!" she would say, if Polly and Lily laughed too uproariously over a silly game, or rushed downstairs to feed lump sugar to the rag-and-bone man's horse. *Decorum* meant always being polite, always being mild and quiet and ladylike, never making a stir. *Boys* didn't have to worry about decorum. Maurice and the other St. Dunstan's boys were allowed to shout, to kick balls, to have rough play-fights. It wasn't that Polly actually wanted to do those things; it just seemed unfair that boys could do so much more.

"You know," Polly had remarked to Lily once, "I really wish *I'd* been a boy!"

"Well, *I* don't," Lily retorted. "Imagine not being able to wear nice clothes or hair ribbons, or have pretty things! You mean you'd rather be Maurice?"

"Well, no, not *Maurice* –"

"And you can't do anything about it, so what's the point of wishing?" Lily had pointed out.

Polly couldn't help thinking, sometimes, that Lily was exactly the sort of daughter Mama wanted – pretty and neat, always polite and respectful. Lily's fair hair, of which she was very proud, was always brushed and shining, not plain, dull brown like Polly's. Now Mama had invited into her drawing room a young woman who cared nothing for decorum, who had attacked a policeman outside Buckingham Palace, and had been a prisoner at Holloway! It would almost be funny, if Polly didn't care so much about being friends with Edwina and Violet. Because they did seem to be her friends, surprising though it was; they had actually said so. They had far more important things to bother about, yet they bothered with *her*.

She had to prove herself worthy of them by persisting with her hunger strike.

At breakfast time, still yawning after her broken night, she said that she didn't want any of the porridge Mrs. Parks was preparing in the kitchen. The sideboard was set temptingly with pots of jam and honey, and the salty smell of Papa's breakfast kippers lingered, but Polly made herself say, "I don't want any porridge, thank you, Mrs. Parks. I'm not hungry."

Mama heard, of course. She was getting so big now, with the baby inside her, that she could only just fit between the dining table and the sideboard. "Oh, Polly! Are you feeling queasy? Dizzy? I do hope you're not going down with something." She placed a cool hand on Polly's forehead. "You don't feel as if you're running a temperature – but perhaps you ought to stay at home today, just in case. Shall I call Dr. Mayes?"

"No! No, I'm quite all right really," Polly said hastily. Hunger striking would be even harder if she had to spend the day in bed, with nothing to do but think about food. "Just not hungry, that's all."

By lunchtime she felt ravenous, and the meat and potatoes served up in the refectory smelled more delicious than anything she could have imagined. She made herself pretend to pick at her food, then offer it to Maudie Marchant, who was always willing to eat up what anyone else didn't want. She managed to slide her portion on to Maudie's plate without any of the teachers noticing. It was harder to resist apple pie and whipped cream, but she made herself go without, though her stomach gave a rumble of outrage and her greedy eyes devoured every mouthful taken by the girls at her table. Some of them even had seconds. Really, she ought to get extra credit for that – the suffragettes in their prison cells didn't have to watch other people gorging on dessert! She sipped at a glass of water, beginning to feel quite virtuous. If anyone asked why she wasn't eating, she could say she was excited about the summer vacation beginning this week.

The walk home seemed twice as long as usual. On the corner of Pimlico Road, the news vendor's billboard said that an Austrian Archduke had been shot dead in Sarajevo. It sounded rather exciting.

"Where's Sarah-jeevo?" Polly asked the vendor, balancing on one leg while she removed a stone from her shoe.

The man shrugged. "Balkans, it says, Miss. Never heard of it neever." A pin-striped man, about to walk briskly past, glanced at the board and stopped, handing over a coin. Polly retied her shoelace and trudged on home.

Her legs ached wearily as she climbed the stairs. Mrs. Parks was scuttling out of the kitchen, carrying a tray loaded with the best tea set. There were voices in the drawing room, and Mrs. Dalby's tinkling laughter.

Preoccupied with her hollow stomach, Polly had almost forgotten – it was the tea party she had been fearing! She went into her bedroom to put down her bookbag, tidy her hair – the good thing about wearing it in pigtails was that it never really got *untidy* – and wash her hands for tea. Then, feeling very self-conscious, she went to join the grownups. The room was fuller than she had expected – Mrs. Dalby was there, and Edwina, but also Great Aunt Millicent, filling her armchair with a vast puff of frilled organdie, and Great Uncle Victor, thin and mustached, in a tweed suit and tie in spite of the heat of the day, sitting to attention with his walking stick propped in front of him, resting both hands on its silver handle. Polly had barely time to glance at Edwina before Great Aunt Millicent cried, "Polly, dear! Come and give your great aunt a kiss! My, my – what a pretty young lady you're turning into!"

Dutifully, Polly kissed them each in turn – Great

Aunt Millicent smelling of face powder and freesia perfume, Great Uncle Victor of pipe tobacco and coal-tar soap. "Quite the image of your mother!" her great aunt continued. "And she says you're being *such* a help, in her confinement!"

"Am I?" Polly turned to her mother.

"Darling, of course you are." Mama summoned Polly to stand beside her. "Miss Rutherford, I believe you've met my daughter Polly?"

"Yes, indeed. How do you do, Polly?" said Edwina. She was wearing a dress of aquamarine silk with the fashionable square neckline, her fair hair was sleekly dressed, and she looked quite at home in Mama's elegant drawing room – as decorous as Mama could have wished.

"Very well, thank you." Polly felt shy, as if this were a different Edwina from the one she had met before.

"I'm so sorry, Miss Rutherford," Mama said. "I interrupted you. You were telling us about your acquaintance with the Earl of Belmont?"

"Oh yes. You see he's a second or third cousin, or something like that. It was through another cousin of mine, Edward Holdsworth – do you know the Holdsworths of Eaton Square? – that I heard the apartment was to be available. He and the Belmonts know each other from shooting parties, and I've met them myself at the odd dinner party…"

Polly sat on a stool and listened with amazement as Edwina played the part of the perfect drawing-room guest, giving no hint of the passions that drove her. So fascinating was the impersonation that Polly had accepted and eaten a slice of coffee cake before she remembered her hunger strike. She could imagine Mrs. Dalby – and even her mother – at the haberdashery counter of Peter Jones, remarking loudly, "Our new neighbor's a cousin of the Earl of Belmont – our landlord, don't you know. Yes, we had tea together just the other day."

When Edwina had finished explaining about the apartment, Maurice's mother ventured, "What a pity your friend, Miss Cross, wasn't able to join us! Now tell me – I'm not quite clear what her role is. Is she your secretary, maybe?"

Edwina gave a gentle smile. "No – I am not her employer. She is my friend – we share the apartment, and work together."

"Oh! At what kind of work?"

"We are campaigners for women's suffrage," said Edwina.

She spoke matter-of-factly, but Polly's eyes darted quickly around the room to take in everyone's reactions. Mama's hostess smile hardly wavered, but Mrs. Dalby shot her a keen, almost triumphant glance, signaling wait-till-we-discuss-this-later. Great Uncle Victor took a sharp breath, and clutched his walking stick more tightly. "Well!" said Great Aunt Millicent, closing her eyes as if needing to assimilate the news in private.

Mrs. Dalby was first to recover. "And what exactly," she asked, silky-smooth, "might this campaigning consist of?"

CHAPTER SEVEN

That Sort of Person

Gossip, gossip, gossip! It must be Meredith Dalby's favorite pastime, Polly thought. She couldn't imagine anything more pointless.

When everyone left, at the end of the tea party, Mrs. Dalby wished Edwina a cold "good day," and went downstairs, only to return half an hour later. Polly wasn't at all surprised. She guessed the reason: to discuss Edwina with Mama, in private. The two women settled in the drawing room, side by side on the sofa, and Mama rang the bell to order a fresh pot of tea from Mrs. Parks. They never seemed to tire of drinking tea and talking.

"Well, my dear!" Mrs. Dalby told Mama, with a trophy-hunter's relish. "You'll never guess what I've just found out from my Elsie! She's been talking to their maid, and *she* said –"

Polly was supposed to be practicing the piano, but with Mrs. Dalby and Mama in firm occupation of the drawing room, she had the perfect excuse for slacking. The door was ajar; as soon as Mrs. Parks had taken in the tea, Polly stood just outside, anxious not to miss a single word of Mrs. Dalby's revelations.

"Holloway Prison…violent conduct in the street, attacking a policeman, if you can believe it!" Mrs. Dalby went on, in shocked delight.

"Meredith! No!"

"It's true, I assure you! Only out on license… may well end up back there…yes, really, my dear!…

A meeting there the other night…posters and leaflets everywhere, a sort of headquarters…well, who knows? Weapons, a bomb factory? You know some of these women will stop at nothing, they're quite fanatical… What if the police raid the premises?… She's been completely disowned by her parents, Elsie told me… they're related to the Rutherfords at Kew…and I can't say I'm the slightest bit surprised… Yes, com*pletely* unsuitable…and enticing Polly up there!"

A startled sound from Mama: Polly shrank back, though her ears strained for what Mrs. Dalby said next.

"Oh yes! Maurice told me. He was with Polly in the garden, when one of them called to her from the window and invited her in, and of course – such a docile little thing she is! – she trotted straight up there."

Polly felt herself going hot all over. *Docile little thing!* She wasn't entirely sure what *docile* meant, but would find out later. As for Maurice – what a tattletale, running straight to his mother to tell on her! She'd have something to say to him tomorrow –

But Mrs. Dalby hadn't finished yet. "My dear, you must put your foot down very firmly! I can't get over the nerve of her, Miss Airs and Graces, sitting there as if butter wouldn't melt in her mouth, going on about the Earl of Belmont! I should think he'd disown her too, if he had the slightest inkling what she's up to! I shall write to him personally…it's quite disgraceful, so inconsiderate to the rest of us… And the other one, who I'm not surprised didn't even show her face, is from the East End. From *Bethnal Green*, my dear! No doubt thinks herself a very clever little minx, wheedling herself into the favors of Her Ladyship up there…"

Polly listened, appalled, barely recognizing Violet and Edwina from these caricatures. Mama, hardly able to get a word in, made occasional murmurs of assent or outrage.

At last there were sounds of Mrs. Dalby rising to her

feet, preparing to leave; quickly Polly scuttled to her bedroom, almost bumping into Mrs. Parks, who said nothing but wagged a finger at her, knowing she'd been eavesdropping.

As soon as the door closed behind Mrs. Dalby, Polly confronted her mother.

"Mama! She came back to tell you things about Edw – about Miss Rutherford," she corrected herself. "Didn't she? I know she doesn't like them – but you can't believe everything she says! You know it's only gossip!"

Mama put a hand to her back. "But how *much* of it is gossip? You know the saying – there's no smoke without fire. Is it true that you went up to Apartment Three, and didn't see fit to tell me about it?"

Polly was silent; Mama gave her a reproachful look. "I'm afraid, darling, it looks as if you haven't been very truthful. Have you? I really don't want you to come into contact with that sort of person. *Most* unfortunate that they live in the same building.

Yes, it was I who invited Miss Rutherford here – but that was before I knew."

"Well," Polly retorted, "I *like* That Sort of Person – far better than I like Mrs. Dalby's Sort of Person. All she does is—"

"*Polly!*" her mother said sharply. "I will not have you speak to me like that, nor show such disrespect to Mrs. Dalby!"

"Sorry," Polly mumbled. But it was true. She did like Violet and Edwina far more than she liked Maurice's mother, even though she'd only just met them. Edwina and Violet were *interesting*! They thought differently from other people. They cared nothing for decorum or what was expected of them. She tried again. "They're my friends! I like them! You're not going to stop me being friends with them, are you?"

"Friends? Now you're just being ridiculous," Mama said sharply. "You've only known them a matter of days. Do you think women like those are likely to be interested in someone your age, a schoolgirl?"

But they *are*, Polly thought mutinously. They *are* interested in me, and not only because I've promised to help them. Nothing could have been more flattering than to be asked. There could be no question of going back on her word.

"We'll wait and see what your father has to say," Mama said firmly. "Now I really must rest, and I suggest you do your piano practice. You've been skimping it lately, haven't you?"

Wait-and-see-what-your-father-has-to-say was usually a bad sign. When he came home from the bank just after six, he and Mama retired to the drawing room with their before-dinner sherry – this time with the door firmly closed. By the time they came out, Papa had made a New Rule.

"Polly, I have told your mother that I will not have you consorting with those women upstairs. If you meet them coming in or out, you may nod, and wish them a polite 'good morning', or 'good afternoon'; but that is all."

"But—"

"Don't answer me back, young lady! I have made a Rule, and I expect you to follow it. If your mother had had any idea what this Miss Rutherford is really like, she would never have considered inviting her into our home. I'm very shocked to hear you've been visiting them without permission – don't let me hear of such a thing again."

At dinner Polly gazed gloomily at her plate. She wasn't hungry; she might as well have gone all day without eating, after all.

"Don't pick at your food, Polly," her mother reproved. "And sit up straight. If you can't be cheerful, at least remember your table manners."

Do this, don't do that. Be a good girl. Do as you're told. Sometimes it seemed this was all she ever heard.

What now? She couldn't let down Edwina and Violet, after promising to help them; couldn't simply say *my parents won't let me.* Not to someone who'd rather go to prison than do as she was told!

*Don't let me hear of such a thing again...*those were Papa's precise words.

Don't let me hear...

The more his phrase echoed in her head, the more it seemed to offer another meaning. Funny, Polly thought, how you could bend words when you tried. Do it, but don't let Papa find out. All right then! Since that was what he wanted...

After dinner she remembered to look up *docile* in Papa's big dictionary.

Easily led or taught, it said; *obedient*.

Puh! went Polly. She slammed the heavy dictionary shut. Obedient? Easily led? We'll see about *that*.

CHAPTER EIGHT

Dog at Heel

For years and years, ever since Polly had started at The Mary Burnet School, she and Lily had been escorted back and forth: at first by their nanny, later by one or other of the mothers. Only for the last year and a half had they been allowed to go unaccompanied. Officially, now that Lily was gone, Polly was supposed to walk to school and back with Maurice, but she usually tried to avoid him. This was easy to do, as the way in and out of the second- and third-floor apartments was from Flood Street at the side. Only the Dalbys' first-floor apartment had the grand Chelsea Walk entrance, through the iron gates and up the steps to the massive front door. Mama sighed with envy over Apartment Number One's splendor, but Polly preferred being on the second floor, at tree-height, even if it meant going in and out the side way.

Although she tried to give Maurice the slip, he sometimes lurked in wait for her. On Tuesday morning, in Royal Hospital Road, he ran up behind her and tugged at one of her pigtails.

"You'd better watch it, Pegs, being friends with jailbirds! It might be infectious!" He was still panting from the run to catch her up.

"Better stay away from me, then," Polly said crossly, straightening her straw boater. "Anyway, that's all *you* know."

"It's true! My mother said!"

"Your mother doesn't know everything. She makes

half of it up if you ask me, just to have something to gossip about." Dodging around a dairy cart, Polly crossed to the other side of the road, but Maurice trotted behind her like a spaniel at heel. She rounded on him, remembering. "And what she doesn't know, *you* tell her! Why are you such a beastly tattletale? Had you run out of slugs and toads to play with?"

Maurice stared at her open-mouthed. "Well, I didn't know it was telling tales! How was I to know you weren't supposed—"

"Aren't you a bit old to be telling your mother everything?" Polly was in no mood to listen. "Does she have to tell you what to think? Mind your own business, next time! And your Elsie's just as bad, spreading rumors—"

"It's *all* of our business, my mother says – we live in the same house. All the same," Maurice said, kicking a stone along the gutter, "it's a lot more interesting than your friend lily-white, living with jailbirds!"

"I wish Lily could have stayed, and *you'd* moved

out!" Polly marched on, hoping to shake Maurice off, especially when she saw two other boys in dung-brown blazers standing by the entrance to the Royal Hospital Gardens.

"I wonder if they'll –" he began, still at her shoulder, keeping pace.

She surprised him into silence by turning abruptly to face him. "Good dog, Maurice! *Here*, boy!" she called, loudly enough for the other boys to hear. "Sit! *Good* boy!"

"Oh, what're –"

The two boys had heard, just as she planned, and now Maurice was the center of attention. "*Ruff! Ruff!*" barked the taller boy, while the other held up his hands like paws, and lolled his tongue out, panting. Maurice's face turned bright red, clashing horribly with his ginger hair.

Ha! Served him right. Abandoning him to their taunts, Polly marched on toward Norton Terrace.

By the end of the afternoon, turning into Wellington Square for her music lesson with Mrs. Langrish, Polly couldn't help but feel optimistic. It was the vacation – weeks and weeks of it stretched ahead, day after long summer day. And, in August, a seaside vacation in Folkestone; that would be fun. Meanwhile, at home, no one could watch her every minute of the day, and it wasn't as if she had to escape from the house to see Violet and Edwina – only tiptoe up the stairs, or talk to them in the garden.

Polly thought of Mrs. Langrish as Aunt Dorothy, even though she was Lily's aunt, not hers. She lived in one of the elegant white houses that lined Wellington Square, off the King's Road. She was waiting on the doorstep, waving a folded sheet of notepaper.

"Polly! I saw you coming down the Square. Such wonderful news!"

Polly had always liked Lily's aunt. A widow with no children of her own, she doted on her niece, and loved planning picnics, outings and surprise treats. She was small, lively and round-faced – probably older than Mama, with little lines around her eyes, but she was so full of enthusiasm that you could easily think she was younger. "Look! This letter came this morning!" She flourished it gaily. "Dear Lily's coming to stay, in two weeks, for a whole week! Isn't that marvelous – I know you must be missing her even more than I am. You can read what she says before we start our lesson."

Aunt Dorothy wasn't nearly as strict a piano teacher as Polly's parents liked to imagine, and only scolded Polly very mildly for her lack of practice when she blundered through the mazurka she was supposed to have learned. "We'll try again next week, and you can practice every day in the meantime. Lily will have been doing even less, if I know her. We're going to have such fun when she comes to stay!"

An hour later, arriving home, Polly found a letter awaiting her, from Lily, with the same news.

"That will cheer you up!" said Mama, who was obviously trying to pretend that yesterday hadn't happened. *It'll put that suffragette nonsense out of your head!* she was quite obviously thinking, as clearly as if a caption had unscrolled itself in the air above her.

Polly's view was different. Lily would be her ally, and it would be just as if she had never gone away. Polly might have to do a bit of persuading, but she and Lily always did things together, whenever they could. With Lily staying, there would be all sorts of excuses for outings and picnics. Hyde Park was the obvious place for a picnic, wasn't it? And maybe Polly would just happen to discover that she had a banner packed with her sandwiches instead of a napkin: a banner of purple, white and green.

CHAPTER NINE

Quarrel

"I've come to help with the banners," Polly said, at the door to Apartment Three.

It was Edwina who had answered her ring. "Hello, Polly! Good of you to come back so soon." She didn't seem at all surprised; but then she didn't know what a dreadful gossip Mrs. Dalby was, or how indiscreet Kitty had been. In the drawing room, she pulled out a large fabric-stuffed bag from behind an armchair.

"Violet's in charge of this really, but I know she's cut out some letters ready. Here are some of the banners, already sewn together." She pulled out a broad band, made from long strips of purple and green. "The letters are white, you see – they'll spell out VOTES FOR WOMEN, and WE DEMAND THE RIGHT TO VOTE. You'd better pin the letters on first, to get the spacing right. Here's Violet's sewing box" – she flipped open the lid – "with everything you need. Will you excuse me while I finish this article? I must get it in the mail for tomorrow. Then I'll sew with you."

"I can't stay long." Polly glanced at the clock on the mantelpiece. "Mama rests this time of day, and –" She stopped, not wanting to say that she was forbidden to be here. Edwina glanced at her, and she said instead: "Such good news – Lily's coming to stay, in two weeks! My best friend Lily, whose apartment this used to be."

"How lovely! I shall invite you both to tea," Edwina said at once. "I'll ask Kitty to bake a special cake."

"It's very kind of you," Polly said formally; but her brain was churning over the new problem this created. How could she bring Lily to tea, when she wasn't allowed here herself? And in any case, wouldn't Lily hate to see her apartment, her own bedroom, all changed and cluttered with other people's things? And what would Edwina think of Lily, with her good-girl manners and her love of pretty things?

"That's settled, then. I shall look forward to it!" Edwina moved to the writing desk in the corner, which was arranged like a small office, with an upright chair, typewriter, and stacks of box files and papers.

While Polly sorted out fabric letters and pinned them to the banner, Edwina bashed the keys at furious speed, occasionally breaking off with a "Blast!" when she made a mistake. (Mama would be shocked about that, too – a lady, cursing like a workman!) Fascinated, Polly kept glancing at her. Perhaps Edwina earned money by working at home, doing people's typing for them? A record was playing from a gramophone on the floor, the music punctuated by the uneven clatter of keys, the ting of the bell at the end of each line, and the swoosh as Edwina tugged back the carriage.

"There!" Edwina said at last, pulling out her final sheet of paper.

"Is this what you do?" Polly looked up from threading a needle. "Secretary work?"

"No, it's journalism. I write articles for various newspapers. It's a way of spreading the word, you see. I take every opportunity I can."

"Oh!" Polly felt out of her depth. Writing for newspapers! It sounded very impressive: maybe Edwina wrote pieces in *The Times* newspaper Papa read every day! But if they were about votes for women, he wouldn't read them – just huff, and turn to the business pages.

"What do you want to do when you leave school, Polly?" Edwina said, rummaging in the bureau drawers.

Polly hesitated; then said in a rush, "I want to be an

explorer. I know it's silly, and Mama says girls can't be explorers—"

"Of course they can," Edwina said sharply. "What about Mary Kingsley? What about Gertrude Bell? Women have traveled through Mesopotamia, climbed mountains in the Himalayas. Can't be explorers? Try telling *them* what they can and can't do!"

"Mama and Papa want to send me to Switzerland, to a finishing school. Doesn't it sound funny, being *finished*? It means learning all about manners, and how to give dinner parties, and what to say when you meet a duke or a countess."

"I know. My parents would have sent me to one, but I refused to go. Schools for young ladies!" Edwina gave her horse-like *hrrrumph*. "Finished! Finished as an independent human being, more like! Education, that's what girls need. Exactly the same education as boys. The same opportunities. If you want to be an explorer, Polly, that's what you should be. Where do you want to go?"

"Oh –" Polly thought of all the countries in the atlas and on the globe, the places her finger had landed. "Africa. Antarctica. India. Australia. Little islands right out in the Pacific Ocean. It's just that – when you look at the world, and see what a small place England is, it seems silly to stay here all your life, just because you happen to be born here, when there are all these other, different places!"

"You're absolutely right there. I must lend you a favorite book of mine – you'll love it, I'm sure. Just a moment –" Edwina left the room, but kept calling out questions from along the hallway: "What's your favorite subject at school, Polly? What are you good at? What don't you like? Have you got good teachers?"

At first Polly called back her answers: "Geography. I'm best at that, and at art, and I quite like games, except in winter. I'm hopeless at math and French. I can never remember how irregular French verbs go, and Mam'selle gets so impatient –" After a few minutes of this, as Edwina showed no sign of coming back, Polly followed her.

"Here it is! Knew it was here somewhere." Edwina emerged from one of the bedrooms, holding out a book in a red cover. Polly looked, and read: *Under Desert Skies: the Journal of a Female Traveler*, by Olive Kingston.

"Take it. Borrow it. And anything else you like the look of," Edwina said, brushing dust off her hands.

"May I?" Polly flicked through the pages, handling the book carefully. "Thank you!" She looked up, and past Edwina at shelves and shelves of books that took up a whole wall of the bedroom. This used to be Lily's room, and there had been only one small shelf above the bed; Edwina must have had these put up specially. "Are they all yours?"

"Have a look." Edwina waved an airy hand. "Borrow as many as you like. I've just got to write a quick letter, then we'll both get on with the sewing."

"I've just remembered something," Polly said.

"About the girl who used to live here – the one who planted the walnut tree. She wanted to be a gardener, and people told her it wasn't a job for a girl, but now she is one. Was, rather, because she's old now, and retired. But she worked as Head Gardener at a big house in Sussex. Mrs. Parks told me, because Miss Frazer – I think that was her name – called to see the house, and her walnut tree, when she came to the Flower Show at the Royal Hospital last year."

Edwina looked delighted. "Well, there you are! A wonderful example here in this very house."

She returned to her typing. Polly knew she should be going back downstairs, but couldn't resist; she went into the bedroom and moved along the shelves, touching the spines of books, reading the titles. It was like a private library! Poetry; novels; history; lots of books about politics and the rights of women. No wonder Edwina was so clever, if she'd read all these…

She was looking at *The Mill on the Floss* when she heard a key turn in the lock, and someone entered in a hurry. Violet, it must be. Polly was replacing the book, about to go into the hallway and say hello, when Violet's angry voice made her jump.

"Edwina, I thought you'd promised! A fool, I am, to believe what you say – I *thought* I heard the door, in the middle of the night! Agnes told me – you went sneaking out to break windows, didn't you? It's lucky you're still here, not in Holloway Prison! Only I suppose that's what you want, really?"

Edwina answered, with perfect calmness: "We've got to keep up the pressure. I can't bear to sit about doing nothing."

Violet had marched into the drawing room, but her voice was loud and clear. "It's like a sport to you, though, en't it? Breaking windows under the noses of the police. You're addicted to it!"

"Nonsense!"

"And you haven't got your strength back, not yet," Violet persisted. "Will you promise me – and I mean really promise this time – not to go out again at night?"

"I'll promise nothing of the sort." Edwina sounded haughty now. "Could you stop shouting, please? You're giving me a headache – and Polly's here."

This was Polly's cue to slink back and join them, red-faced and embarrassed to find herself overhearing such a quarrel.

"Oh, hello, Polly," said Violet, attempting a smile; but then she rounded on Edwina again, evidently too full of outrage to hold it in. "When it comes down to it, it's votes for ladies you're fighting for, en't it? For upper-class ladies. For you and your sort. Not votes for the ordinary working women where I come from – the East Enders, the factory workers, the wives struggling to make ends meet, with five kids and a drunken husband – the ones we really need. How are they meant to make themselves heard?"

Edwina looked at her exasperatedly. "We've got to be single-minded, don't you see that? We can't get sidetracked into all sorts of other causes."

"It's got to be for *every*one, not some sort of – of

personal triumph!" Violet stomped over to the window, and stood for a moment leaning on the sill, while Polly looked anxiously from her to Edwina and back again; Edwina, quite composed, addressed an envelope and stuck on a stamp. Kitty came in, raised her eyebrows, then, catching Polly's glance, gave a conspiratorial half-grin, as if she were quite used to spats like these.

"Oh, Kitty," said Edwina, "are you making tea?"

"Nearly ready," Kitty replied; "crumpets, too, if you want."

"Ooh, I should think so. Do we?" Edwina looked at Polly, then at Violet.

Violet wasn't going to be sidetracked by crumpets. "You know, I sometimes wonder if we're fighting for the same thing at all! Sometimes I wonder how much you understand. That chaise long-ew you bought on a whim the other day – that'd be six months' housekeeping for my mum!"

"*Chaise longue,*" Edwina corrected, in an emphatically French accent.

Violet looked exasperated. "Oh, Edie, you're such a terrible snob!"

Polly held her breath: how could Violet *say* such things? But, to her amazement, Edwina burst out laughing.

"Yes, you're quite right! Just listen to me! How terribly prissy I am! Let's have tea and crumpets and forget all about our differences."

Violet began to laugh too, and Kitty rolled her eyes at the ceiling and turned for the kitchen.

"Sorry, Polly. You must think we're a pair of alley cats, spitting and scratching!" said Violet, settling herself on the despised chaise longue. "We're not always like this, fortunately. Oh, you've made a start on the sewing!" she added, noticing Polly's work – a V and an O tacked, none too neatly, to a strip of purple and green.

"Yes. But I think I'd better go home now," Polly said awkwardly.

"What, and miss the crumpets? Not because of my

little temper tantrum, I hope?" Violet pulled a rueful face.

"No – it's just that I'm expected."

"Thank you, Polly," said Edwina from her desk. "We're very grateful."

It was Violet who went with her to the door. "Do come again – whenever you like!" she called, as Polly crept down the stairs.

Polly hoped she hadn't spoken loudly enough for Mama to hear. She slid through the front door of Apartment Two, which she had left unlocked.

She felt shocked by the vehemence of the argument – almost shaking. Edwina and Violet were behaving now as if nothing had happened; but how could they disagree so strongly, and still be friends?

CHAPTER TEN

Reasons

Next morning, Polly let herself out into the garden before anyone else was up, even before Mrs. Parks had arrived in the kitchen. She liked to be outside in the early morning: she liked the damp smell of grass and earth, the sense of everything waking up to the day, a wood pigeon cooing in the top of the walnut tree, and the sounds of hooves and wheels in Oakley Street beyond the old mews, which gave her the smug feeling of having a day of leisure ahead of her while the rest of London busied itself with shops and offices and delivery rounds.

She glanced up at the top floor. Perhaps the quarrel last night hadn't been as bad as she thought it at the time. Violet's outburst might be better than the way Papa and Mama went about it, on the rare occasions when they disagreed – not so much an exchange of views as a cooling of the air that spread chillily through the whole apartment, so that Polly felt numbed by it.

With her special notebook, Lily's leaving present, she sat on the swing. The seat was wet with dew; immediately she felt dampness through her skirt and petticoats, but it was too late to worry about that now.

Lily's notebook had marbled covers and a silk ribbon bookmark. At first Polly had thought she might write a story in it; but as no story had come to her, she now decided to use it for Plans and Ideas. It would have to be kept secret, of course; she would hide it under her pillow, wrapped in her nightgown.

Plans and Ideas, she wrote carefully on the first page. *Find out about being an explorer. Read "Under Desert Skies" and lots of other books.* Then, on page two, a heading: *Ten Reasons why Maurice shouldn't have the vote.*

She sucked the end of her pencil, then went on:

1. *He tells tales.*
2. *He is rude.*
3. *He treads on ants.*
4. *He pulls girls' hair and knocks their hats off in the street.*
5. *He took the last jam tart at teatime without asking if anyone else wanted it.*
6. *He thinks he knows everything.*
7. *He stole Lily's doll and threw her up in the tree and laughed when she got caught by her hair.*
8. *He is a horrible, slimy, nasty, unkind <u>boy</u>.*

9. *He thinks boys are better than girls.*
10. *He will be even worse by the time he is a grownup and old enough to vote.*

There! she thought with satisfaction, drawing a squiggly line underneath. That was Maurice summed up!

"Morning, Polly!"

It was Violet, coming out from the back-stairs entrance with a basket of laundry under her arm, making for the washing line at the end of the garden, which was separated from the lawn by a bed of shrubs.

Polly darted across. "Let me help!"

"You're out early – what a glorious day!" Violet propped the heavy basket against one hip. "Just putting these out before I go off to work." She looked so cheerful that Polly could hardly believe she was the same person who'd ranted at Edwina last night. She couldn't decide which of the two young women she liked best: Violet, for her kindness and ordinariness, or Edwina, so clever and determined. Just imagine, going out on a window-smashing raid, after a demure tea with Mama and Mrs. Dalby!

According to Papa, Polly should have said a stiff "good morning," and gone straight indoors.

"I'm not supposed to talk to you," she confided. "And now Edwina says she'll invite me and Lily to tea – that's my best friend Lily who used to live in your flat. Only we won't be allowed!"

"Oh?"

"It's Papa, you see. He's terribly strict." Polly explained about Papa's New Rule, while they pegged out the blouses and undergarments (she could just imagine Mrs. Dalby having something to say about *that*, if she ventured this far down the garden: "How utterly shameless! Underclothes hanging on a washing line, for the whole world to see! Did you ever hear the like?")

Violet listened in concern, then said, "I wouldn't want to stir up trouble for you, with your ma and pa. Shame though – just when we was getting to know one another! Can't you talk to your pa – convince him we're really quite human?"

"I don't know," Polly said doubtfully. Papa was not really open to negotiation, once he'd made his views known.

"Anyway, that's a job done. Thank you," said Violet, when the washing was pegged jauntily on the line. "We'll find a way, somehow or other. You can always blame it on me if your pa finds out."

"But I want to carry on helping with the banners and leaflets!" They were walking slowly back up the garden.

"Well, you know you're always welcome – whenever you can come up for the odd half hour. You know the old saying, *What the eye doesn't see, the heart doesn't grieve over*?"

Polly considered. That did sound rather like her own thinking; but it hadn't stopped Violet from being angry when Edwina slipped out of their apartment without telling her. It sounded fine as a saying, but she wasn't sure how well it would work.

Violet paused, seeing the notebook on the swing seat where Polly had left it. "That yours? Are you writing a story?"

"No, not a story." Polly fetched it. "Here. I did this." She handed over the open book and stood self-consciously while Violet read the list, sure now that it was a very childish thing to have done.

Violet laughed. "Poor Maurice! You can't blame him for being a boy, you know! He can't help that, and there are some very nice ones about!"

"Are there?" Polly said. "I'm afraid I don't know any."

Violet looked at her. "Don't go thinking we hate men, you know, just 'cos we stand up for women's rights. Well, there's some might do, but I en't one of them. There's men in our movement, too – male suffragists!"

"Oh!" said Polly, confused.

"One of them, Mr. Pethick-Lawrence, even went to prison and went on a hunger strike. You see, Poll, you don't have to be a woman to think us women deserve the vote. Any more'n you have to be poor to think people shouldn't have to starve," Violet explained. "Fair-minded people want the best for everyone."

"Doesn't *every*one want the best for everyone?"

"It would be nice if they did. But lots of folk's only interested in themselves."

She was about to go indoors; Polly hesitated, then said, "Violet?"

"Mm?"

"Yesterday – you know, the – the argument."

"Oh, that." Now it was Violet's turn to look embarrassed. "You mustn't take any notice of us. Go at each other hammer and tongs, we do, sometimes."

"It sounded as if – as if you don't really like each other."

Violet grinned. "Sometimes I could wring Edwina's neck! But it's not because I don't like her. She's been so good to me, and I admire her for what she does, even if I don't always agree. It's the risks she takes, the way she drives herself! But we're in this together – always have been, always will be."

Polly smiled with relief. Really! The peculiar ways grownups behaved! At least with Maurice she knew what to expect.

"Sometimes, you know," Violet went on, "the people you care about most, are the ones you get most angry with. Best go now, or I'll make meself late." Violet turned for the side door, but added over her shoulder, "That list of yours – how about 'Ten reasons why Polly *should* have the vote!'"

Yes, of course. Polly sat on the swing again, and began at once with the new heading.

1. *I think I want the best for everyone, not just for myself.*
2. *I can sometimes be sensible.*
3. *I am loyal to my friends.*
4. *I*

Then, defeated, she paused and sucked her pencil. It would be easier to think of bad things about herself, really: I am not very good at arithmetic. I don't always try hard enough at school. I don't think Mama and Papa can trust me not to do things they wouldn't like if they knew about them.

CHAPTER ELEVEN

Lily

The weather continued hot and sunny, as if it had no intention of ever changing; Polly counted the days to Lily's visit, helping Aunt Dorothy to plan outings and surprises. To mark the start of summer vacation, Mr. and Mrs. Dalby took Maurice and Polly on a boat trip along the Thames, all the way from Chelsea to Greenwich. Gazing from the deck, Polly imagined herself voyaging to hidden reaches of the Amazon, or traveling down the Nile to see pyramids and camels. She forgot to wear her hat, and her nose came out in a sprinkling of freckles, which Mama dabbed with lemon juice to make them fade.

It seemed impossible for Mama to get any bigger, but the baby bulge continued to swell. Feeling, she said, like a galleon in full sail, Mama wore loose, light garments, but the heat made her uncomfortable. She fanned herself as she moved slowly about the apartment and garden, saying that she could not wait for Folkestone, and the sea breezes. Polly had to remind herself that Mama's normal size and shape would eventually be restored; it seemed so unlikely. The baby was due at the beginning of August, and the doctor visited regularly, proclaiming that all was well, diagnosing rest and plenty of fluids. Polly hoped the baby would come early, while Lily was here; then maybe she and Lily could take it for walks in its carriage and pretend to be grownup aunties.

The good thing about Mama resting so much was

that Polly could make several escapes to the apartment upstairs, each time with a thrill of defiance. "I thought Violet told me you weren't allowed?" said Edwina; but Edwina, of all people, did not let other people tell her how to behave, so she understood. Polly finished off a whole banner by herself, VOTES FOR WOMEN, and pasted posters to boards which could be carried high. It became her secret project, escaping up the stairs every afternoon if she could. As Violet was out at work at these times, only Edwina was there, and Kitty, who sometimes helped. Occasionally other people called in – usually ladies, but once there was a young man named Leonard, who must be one of the male suffragists Violet had told her about. Certainly, he spoke with just as much certainty and determination as Edwina did.

"I'm definitely going to be a proper suffragette as soon as I'm old enough," Polly announced one afternoon.

"I hope," Edwina said, looking at her over the top of the spectacles she wore for sewing, "it won't be *necessary* to be a suffragette by the time you're grownup. If women haven't got the vote by then, I shall be very disappointed. You must be a traveler, and come home whenever it's time to vote."

"Mama thinks it's a game," Polly said, "me wanting to be an explorer. Like believing in fairies, something I'll grow out of. She thinks I'll be a wife and mother, just like her. But I don't think I'd be very good at it. Wouldn't you like that?" she added; after all, Edwina was the right sort of age, and so was Violet. "I mean, as well as all the other things you do, of course."

"I would only like it," Edwina said, snipping a thread, "if I met exactly the right man. And I haven't, yet. I don't have time to think about it. Now, what about tea with Lily? Shall we say next Thursday?"

Polly colored up. "I'm not sure. We're going to be very busy, you see, with Aunt Dorothy."

Edwina shot her a shrewd glance. "Oh. Of course, you're not supposed to consort with a lawbreaker. How silly of me."

Polly nodded, her face hot.

"What a shame." Edwina was sewing on a letter F, with quick darts of her needle. "Well, tell me about Lily. What's she like? What does she want to do when she grows up?"

"Lily *does* want to get married and have children," Polly said confidently. "Four, she wants. But apart from that, she'd like to be a nurse. I should think she'd make a good nurse."

"But perhaps she could be a *doctor*!" Edwina said at once. "Why shouldn't she be?"

"Because girls don't –" Polly began, already knowing how Edwina would respond.

"But girls *will*! One day, Polly, when we achieve our aims, women will have exactly the same chances and choices as men do. Isn't that only right and fair? Think of you and Maurice – you're just as clever, aren't you? Just as sensible? Just as capable of learning new things?"

"Yes. Yes, I am." Polly had never met anyone who

spoke as Edwina did – who made her feel that anything was possible, that she could choose whatever she wanted from a whole world of opportunities.

Polly returned, as usual, just in time before Mama stirred from her afternoon rest, and blinked at her vaguely. "Oh, there you are, darling! I do hope you're not getting bored."

"Oh, not at all, Mama," Polly answered, innocent-faced.

For now, there was one opportunity she wanted more than any other – she must find a way of going on next Saturday's march! After all, she had folded the leaflets, sewn the sashes, pasted the posters – she was almost a part of it, now. How feeble it would be to miss the event itself! But Mama and Papa would never let her go, that was for certain.

At last the long-awaited day came – the day of Lily's arrival. Lily was to travel up by train, accompanied by her father, as her mother was reluctant to leave

Tunbridge Wells for the heat and smoke of London. Polly, desperate to go and meet them at Victoria so as not to miss a single second of Lily's visit, was told that her parents couldn't allow her to loiter in the station on her own, and of course Mama couldn't think of going all that way in the heat. The only solution was to persuade Maurice to go with her, "as your escort" was the way Mama put it, though Polly thought of him more as cumbersome baggage. As Maurice liked trains and stations, he agreed quite readily; and they managed to walk all the way to Victoria with only one small argument breaking out, about whether or not Maurice would be able to go on a hunger strike and submit to force-feeding, the way Edwina had on her first spell in Holloway.

"I can't see what would be so bad about it," Maurice stated. "All you'd have to do would be lie there. I've had a tooth out, and it can't be nearly as bad as that."

"That's all you know! Violet told me – because

Edwina told *her*, though she's never talked to me about it – it was the most awful agony. Can you imagine? Having tubes forced down your throat and into your stomach, nearly choking you – people holding you down so you can't even struggle, then horrible stuff like gruel pumped in – and the tubes ripped out again afterwards? It was the prison doctor doing it, only you'd never have thought so from how rough he was, Violet said. Edwina only had it once, but some of the suffragettes have had it done to them time and time again. Don't you think they were brave?"

"Brave, or stupid? None of them *had* to have force-feeding – they could have given in and eaten for themselves. They want to make themselves martyrs, that's what my mother says!"

"You have to be brave to be a martyr," Polly said stubbornly.

Maurice was silent for a moment; then, to her surprise, he said, "Yes. All right, then. They *are* brave, to go through all that when they didn't have to."

He had surprised her in another way, too. Two days ago, in the garden, she had boasted to him about her afternoon visits to the apartment upstairs. The moment the words were out of her mouth, she had regretted it; but Maurice had not, apparently, said a word to his mother. Polly was forced to think that maybe even Maurice had his good points.

They reached Victoria, and found the right platform. "I do hope they haven't missed their train!" fretted Polly; but there, already, was Lily, waving, and walking as fast as she could toward the barrier, outpacing her father, who was struggling with a number of bags and cases.

"Polly! Polly!"

The two girls hugged; when they broke apart, Lily said, "Oh, hello, Maurice. I didn't know you'd be here."

"Maurice came with me," Polly explained, "otherwise Mama wouldn't have let me come."

Lily was wearing a new dress of kingfisher blue,

with a low waist and a white collar; her well-brushed fair hair was caught back in matching turquoise ribbons. Polly couldn't help thinking that she already looked a little taller and more grownup than when they had last met; was that possible, in such a short time?

"She's brought enough luggage for a whole family for a month," Lily's father said cheerfully, catching up.

Everything was stowed in a taxicab; then all four of them took their seats and were conveyed in style to Wellington Square.

"Er, I might as well go home, then," Maurice said awkwardly, while Mr. Bradshaw paid the cab driver, and Aunt Dorothy came out to greet the arrivals with cries of delight. Polly had almost forgotten about him.

"Oh, do come and join us for tea!" cried Aunt Dorothy, but Maurice said that he was expected at home, and slipped away.

Shortly afterwards, Lily's father left to catch his train back, and now Lily and Polly could talk properly

– about Lily's new school, and what it was like living in Tunbridge Wells, with the shops and the Pump Room and the Common, and how tedious Polly was finding Maudie Marchant, and the novelty of having suffragettes living upstairs.

"Oh, how exciting!" exclaimed Aunt Dorothy. "I do so admire them!"

"My mother doesn't. Neither does Mrs. Dalby," said Polly. "But *I* do. They're my friends, you know," she added importantly.

"Now, girls," Aunt Dorothy swept on, "we've got so many lovely things to look forward to! I'm getting tickets for *Swan Lake* – we can all go, you too, Polly –"

"It's going to be such fun!" Lily couldn't keep still. "Polly, come up and see my room. You can help me unpack my things."

At last they were alone together: just like old times, when they'd giggled and chattered in Lily's bedroom or Polly's, trying on their mothers' hats, pretending to be very grand, and striking poses in front of the mirror. Aunt Dorothy's spare bedroom was very pretty and girlish, as if decorated specially for Lily: white candlewick bedspreads; curtains patterned with rosebuds, and matching cushions; a bedside lamp in clouded glass, shaped like a bluebell flower. "Two beds!" said Lily, bouncing down on one and kicking up her feet. "Maybe you could come and stay – wouldn't that be fun?" Quickly she sprang up again: "I must hang up my new dress before it gets creased."

From her suitcase she produced more things Polly hadn't seen before: a party dress in ruby velvet, and pretty shoes to go with it, with jet-button fastenings. "For going to concerts and smart occasions like that," she explained.

"You've got a lot of new clothes," Polly remarked. She couldn't help feeling that Lily had overtaken her, and was rushing on into grownup-ness.

"Well, there are such lovely shops in Tunbridge Wells! Just wait till you come and see them. Your dress is quite nice too, Polly. Now tell me all about these suffragettes! I do hope I'll meet them!"

Before Polly knew what time it was, Papa arrived to collect her on his way home from the bank, and she and Lily had to say goodbye to each other until tomorrow.

"I hope you thanked Maurice for going with you to the station?" Papa said, in Flood Street.

Polly felt herself going hot. She hadn't said a word in thanks. She had hardly even said goodbye to him, so eager had she been to hear all Lily's news – and after he had behaved quite nicely, for once. "I'll go and see him now," she mumbled.

While Papa went in at the side entrance, Polly went around to the front, through the gates, and rang the Dalbys' bell. It was Elsie, the gossip, who answered. Polly gave her a stony look, and asked for Maurice.

Elsie showed her in: across the tiled hall that Mama so envied, and up the stairs that led nowhere. There was a halfway landing here, then three stairs that led straight into a blank wall. Before the house had been converted into apartments, this had been the grand stairway leading to all the floors. Now, the landing was an odd in-between place, a dead end, a sort of hidey-hole, and Maurice often left out his games here, or his chess set. He was busy lining up two armies of model soldiers: one side in bright scarlet, the other in royal blue, facing each other across the Turkish red carpet.

"Maurice." Polly paused two stairs short of the landing, and cleared her throat. "I came to say, you know, thank you for coming to the station."

Maurice looked up from his maneuvers, puzzled, as if he'd already forgotten about it. "Oh, that's all right. Hey, Pegs, what d'you think of the news?"

"What news?"

"There's going to be a *war*!" he announced. "My father says so!"

"In Ireland?"

"No. In Europe. Haven't you seen the newspapers?"

"No."

"Well, you should look at them, then. You know about the shooting of the Archduke of Austria a couple of weeks ago?"

"In that place called – what was it – Sarah-something?" Polly remembered the newsstands.

"You mean Sarajevo, in the Balkans."

"Why does that mean there's got to be a war?"

"You wouldn't understand." Maurice gave her one of his lofty, *you're only a girl* looks that made Polly want to hit him.

"Go on, then! Tell me why, if you know all about it!"

Maurice sat back, folding his arms. "Well, it's complicated. My father says Austria is looking for any chance to declare war on Serbia, and this is it. Then it's about all the countries supporting each other, like teams. Germany's on the same side as Austria. Russia will support Serbia. And we'll be in it, too, because we're on the same side as Russia and Serbia. No one can stay out."

"That doesn't sound very likely to me," Polly scoffed.

"All because of one shooting? So this is the war, is it?" She indicated the red and blue armies at her feet. "They're just – dolls for boys, that's all they are!" With her toe, she pushed over two of the royal blues, so that they fell face-down on the carpet.

"It is! You wait and see." Maurice scrambled to pick up his fallen soldiers, his face getting red – the way it did very easily, Polly had noticed. "And if there *is* a war, and it goes on long enough, I'm going to be in it!"

CHAPTER TWELVE

Plotters

Polly was finding it hard to keep up with Lily's new, consuming interest in clothes and fashions. As Aunt Dorothy shared her niece's passion, they spent a whole afternoon in Selfridges, the huge new store, grand as a museum, which Lily and Aunt Dorothy both thought the next thing to Paradise. "Everything under one roof!" marveled Aunt Dorothy. "You could spend all day in here!"

They rode the escalators from floor to floor, gazing at the glittering array of goods for sale, from shoes to chandeliers. "It's like Aladdin's cave!" Polly said, content just to wander; she lingered in the toy department, but Lily dismissed that as "for children" and swept on to *Fashions for the Modern Miss*. Eventually, after much trying on and several changes of mind, Lily bought a hat and a silk shantung dress; Aunt Dorothy bought a blouse, and a box of lace-trimmed handkerchieves for Lily's mother. For the sake of joining in, Polly decided to spend her allowance on new hair ribbons. Dazzled by a rainbow of tempting colors displayed glossily in a drawer, she was about to choose pale lilac, but changed her mind at the last moment and picked green, white and purple.

"You'd have done better with the lavender," Lily remarked. "That was a perfect match for the stripes in your blouse."

"These are suffragette colors! Green for hope, white for purity, purple for dignity."

"I know that! But I don't see why you've wasted your money – you can hardly wear them to school. And your mother won't let you wear them when she's around."

Polly didn't care. The point was to *have* the ribbons – a private expression of her loyalty to Violet and Edwina.

Tired from all the shopping, they had cakes and lemonade in the restaurant, and afterward walked towards Marble Arch, for the bus home.

"Couldn't we go over there, just for a little while?" asked Polly, attracted by the greenness of Hyde Park.

"My feet ache," Lily complained, but Aunt Dorothy thought it was a good idea.

"We can walk down to the Serpentine, and catch a bus from Knightsbridge."

They crossed Park Lane, dodging motorcars and omnibuses, horses and bicycles, and entered the park at what Aunt Dorothy said was Speaker's Corner. Polly looked around her, seeing nothing but a bare space with railings on three sides, and trodden dust.

"Oh! This is where –"

"Yes, that's right," said Aunt Dorothy. "Where anyone can stand up on a soapbox and make a speech."

"Could we do it now?" Polly asked, imagining herself, at this very moment, launching into an address about votes for women. How would people react? There weren't all that many people around to listen – a few strollers, a nursemaid with twins in a carriage, a family having a picnic. How foolish she would feel!

"Well, you could," said Aunt Dorothy, laughing. "But I think there are special times. If you're going to start airing your views, you need an audience. I've heard Mrs. Pankhurst speak here, you know. Very stirring, she was – but there were those in the crowd who booed and jeered at her. A lot of courage, it must take, to stand up and expose yourself to ridicule. I'm quite sure I couldn't do it!"

"You're not a suffragette, are you, Aunt Dorothy?" asked Lily, swinging her shopping bags.

Aunt Dorothy shook her head. "No," she said, with a small sigh. "I half wish I were – I take my hat off to them. But, well, I've got my living to make. Who'd send me their daughters for piano lessons, if I were out on the streets smashing windows and setting buildings on fire?"

"Miss Rutherford's going to make a speech here," Polly said. "Edwina, who I told you about, who lives in Lily's old apartment. And there's going to be a march to Chelsea Town Hall – a parade. It's on Saturday." The idea seized her. "You wouldn't want to miss it, would you?" she appealed to Aunt Dorothy.

"A parade?" said Lily. "We might as well come and see it. Can't we, Auntie?"

"Well, I don't know. Not with my reputation to think of."

"Oh, you don't need to worry about that," Polly assured her. "No one's going to smash windows or set fire to things, not on a *parade*. We could just walk along with them, just for a little way. If we went back to Selfridges and you bought colored ribbons, like mine," she added to Lily, "we could both put them round our straw hats."

"So we'd match, and we could do our hair the same, as well! Yes, do let's!" Lily turned to her aunt. "It would be an awful shame to miss it, when it's so close. We can come, can't we, the three of us?"

Aunt Dorothy still looked doubtful. "Whatever would your parents say?"

"Invite Polly to stay the night," Lily urged her; "then we needn't tell her parents, or mine."

Aunt Dorothy was hesitating, Polly could see. "It would be wrong of me to let you keep secrets from your parents."

Polly had an idea. "I know! We could just happen to be here in the park on Saturday, having a picnic, say, and we'll wander over to see what's going on, and – no one could blame us for that, could they?"

"Go on, Auntie – say yes." Lily put on her most appealing expression, head on one side. "If they *ask*, then we'll tell them – but they won't. No one will mind us having a picnic in the park, and looking at a parade that just happens to be starting off."

"And we won't have to tell even the smallest lie!" added Polly.

"Oh dear, you two!" Aunt Dorothy laughed. "Determined to get me into trouble, the pair of you!"

Polly took a few skipping steps. "Does that mean we can go?"

"Well! I would like to show a bit of support. We'll see."

Did *all* grownups say that? Polly wondered. But there was a difference: when Mama said it, it sounded like No; the way Aunt Dorothy just had, it sounded a lot more like Yes.

It was one of the best weeks Polly could remember. Aunt Dorothy, glad of the girls' company, was quite happy for Polly to spend nearly all the time at Wellington Square. Polly's mother, with the Folkestone trip to plan as well as all the knitting and sewing she was doing for the baby, did not mind her spending so much time with Lily. A visit to Regent's Park Zoo; a tour of the city on an open-topped bus; a tea party with some cousins of Lily's, and *Swan Lake*, which was so beautiful that it brought tears to Polly's eyes, and made Lily decide that she wanted to be a prima ballerina: "I'm going to ask Mama if I can take ballet lessons," she announced. Even Polly daydreamed about pirouetting on a stage and astonishing everyone with her grace, beauty and skill, even though she knew full well that she was far too clumsy.

The week rushed past. At the end of it, like a birthday cake waiting for its candles to be lit, was the march. Busy with Lily and the rush of activity, Polly wasn't able to help with any more preparations, but she did sneak upstairs one morning to push a note under Edwina's and Violet's door: *Good luck for*

Saturday! I will be there at Speaker's Corner and all the way to the Town Hall! Could I have three sashes, please? You could hide them under the blackcurrant bushes.

The very next morning, there were the three bright sashes, tied into a neat package, with a note from Violet: *Well done! I will see you there.*

"I've hardly seen you this week," grumbled Maurice, when Mama sent Polly downstairs with a message for Mrs. Dalby. He was playing chess, by himself, on the landing-space, which struck Polly as a rather pointless thing to do.

"Good job, too!" she retorted. "I expect you've missed having someone to tease."

"Mother says, would you and Lily and her aunt like to come to tea on Sunday?"

"Maybe, if there's time." Polly couldn't think as far as Sunday. Saturday came first, jostling to the front of her mind, blocking out all days beyond. Saturday was a suffragette day, not a red-letter day but a green, white and purple day; the first day of her new career as campaigner for women's rights.

She took the sashes to Wellington Square. Showing them to Lily and Aunt Dorothy made her feel like a proper suffragette.

"I can hardly wait!" Lily kept saying. "It's going to be so *exciting*!"

"Yes, but –" Polly wasn't sure Lily was taking the campaign seriously enough. "It's not just about having fun. It's about standing up for what's right. It's about wanting things to be fair – not wanting to be second-best!"

"I know *that*," Lily said, fingering the sash. "Do you think my white lace blouse would look nice with this? Or the cream one with the sailor collar?"

Aunt Dorothy smiled, and caught Polly's eye. "I don't think you're quite cut out for political campaigning, Lily, somehow!"

"Oh, but I am," Lily protested. "Christabel Pankhurst's *very* fashionable, Mama says. I don't see why one should look a fright when one's marching about the streets – who would take any notice?"

At last Saturday came. Early, Polly packed a small bag with her overnight things.

"I'm wondering if you really need stay overnight with Mrs. Langrish, after all," said Mama, coming into her bedroom. "It's very kind of her, but it puts her to a lot of extra trouble."

"Oh, no," said Polly quickly. "She really doesn't mind at all, and the spare bed's already made up."

"Your father's dining out on Saturday evening, too," Mama said, a little wistfully. "I shall be here all on my own."

"Oh, but I've been so looking forward to it, Mama – and it's Lily's last night, before she goes home!"

Mama sighed. "You're going to miss her," she said gently. "No doubt the two of you want to stay awake talking half the night. Well, I suppose it won't hurt, for once."

Polly felt guilty for deceiving her; but suffragettes

had to make plans, didn't they, secret plans? And, after all, she was only going to walk along a street, not set fire to Mr. Asquith's new golfing villa, or slash a famous painting in the Royal Academy, or throw flour at the Lord Mayor. She knew from Edwina that there were all sorts of plots, more and more of them, ever-ingenious: all to keep the Cause "in the public eye," as Edwina put it.

By the time she left, with Papa carrying her bag, she felt herself almost bursting with concealed excitement. She was going on the march now, and nothing could stop her.

CHAPTER THIRTEEN

Purple, White and Green

"I'm not sure this is such a good idea," Aunt Dorothy said doubtfully.

They were crossing the road toward Speaker's Corner. Already there was quite a gathering, and people were drifting across the park to see what was going on.

"It'll be all right, Auntie," said Lily.

"Well, I hope so. Now, you must stay with me, both

of you, not go running off and getting into trouble."

"As if we would!" Lily gave her an impatient look. "Have you got the sashes, Polly?"

"In the picnic basket."

They stopped by the railings, and Aunt Dorothy took out the three sashes. In her bag she also had the rather simple picnic – cucumber sandwiches, apples and a bottle of lemonade – which was their excuse for being in Hyde Park. Polly felt a swell of pride as she pulled the sash over her head and one arm, and adjusted it against her blouse. Lily, who had finally decided on the white lace, put hers on too, and tilted her hat, with its ribbon band, first one way and then the other.

"Come on! There's no time for primping! I want to see Edwina and Violet." Polly tugged at Lily's arm, moving in the direction of the wooden platform for the speakers; she scanned the faces beneath straw hats decked with suffragette colors. The crowd was mainly women, with only a few men. Among them

Polly recognized Leonard, the young man who had visited Edwina; he was holding a megaphone by his side, and talking earnestly to a tall woman who wore a badge marked *Steward*. Posters on boards, like the ones Polly had helped to make, were stacked against the railings, ready to be held aloft.

Aunt Dorothy had met someone she knew, and was standing talking on the edge of the crowd; Lily was waiting for her, looking toward the platform. Polly moved on, keeping an eye on them. Being in the middle of all this, in the warm sunshine, surrounded by people waving and calling out and greeting each other, felt like being at a party – a very special kind of party. She stood for a moment in a rush of happiness, taking it all in: the sun bright on straw hats and white dresses, the flashes of purple, green and white that linked everyone, the dappled sunshine under the plane trees, the scream of swifts high in the blue, cloud-wisped sky, the clop of hooves on Park Lane, an engine sputtering and the honk of a car horn, someone shouting from a van, the voices around her, the sense of anticipation; she felt she were living as she had never lived before. If I'm going to be a suffragette, she thought, then this is where I'll belong – with women, with people like these, who are prepared to march the streets to stand up for what they believe in.

More and more people were pressing into the area; Lily caught up, grabbing Polly's arm. Polly had to crane her neck to see past the adults surrounding her. Lily, taller, was able to see better, and turned to wave to her aunt: "We're here!" She waved energetically, and Aunt Dorothy pushed her way toward them. "Someone's getting up on the box," Lily reported, "she's going to speak – she's got the megaphone –"

Shushings silenced the crowd, and Polly, craning, saw a tall woman – not Edwina, someone older and more weathered – facing her audience. "Ladies – and gentlemen! May I have your attention, please?" More shushings, fingers held to lips, till all conversations were silenced and everyone faced the speaker. "We of the WSPU," the woman went on, in a loud, confident voice, "are delighted to see such a turnout today – here in Hyde Park, the scene of many glorious rallies in the last few years. In a few minutes we will move off across the park, and on to Sloane Square and the King's Road. Please keep together. I must stress that we want no incident of any kind until we reach Chelsea Town Hall, so please do not respond to any provocation from bystanders. There will be police in attendance, of course, but also our own stewards, who will walk beside and behind the procession. In a moment we will be addressed by one of our comrades who has done so much to organize this march and countless other protests; at the Town Hall there will be more speeches until we are compelled to disperse, while six of our number attempt to enter the building and demand an audience with the Mayor. Thank you again for your support. Now, it is a great honor for me to introduce a most respected member of our sisterhood – Miss Edwina Rutherford."

Applause and cheers broke out as Edwina mounted the box. She seemed to stumble as she stepped up; regained her balance and took the megaphone from the first speaker.

Lily nudged Polly. "Is that her?"

Polly felt so proud that a lump in her throat made it hard to swallow. She nodded, balancing on tiptoe; she fixed her eyes on Edwina, who straightened and paused, surveying the crowd for a few moments without speaking. Then she began: "Thank you, Miss Selby. I would like to add my own thanks to hers for this magnificent turnout." Her voice was quiet and calm; the effect on the audience was that everyone stood hardly moving, focusing their full attention on the slight figure with the megaphone. "Gatherings like these," Edwina continued, "can leave the government in no doubt about the strength of our determination. Petitions with over a million signatures have now been handed in at the House of Commons. Take heed,

Prime Minister Asquith" – she turned, as if sending her words over the heads of her audience in the direction of Westminster – "if you will not listen to us, we will *make* you listen! We will not be ignored; we will never give up the fight. For how can we give up our struggle, go back to being dutiful mothers, daughters, wives and workers, when the government insists on treating us as second-class citizens? When we are—"

"Stand back. Stand back," a loud male voice cut in; there was a surge in the crowd behind Polly, and she turned to see four helmeted policemen pushing toward the front. "Make way. Madam, please stand aside. I must insist you give way."

Edwina must have seen the disturbance, but she carried on, barely faltering: "– when we are denied the rights given to any man who happens to –"

Polly found herself pushed aside, off balance, by the swell of movement, as people tried to push in different directions – some merely trying to get out of the way, others defiantly blocking the path of the policemen. One woman began battering the arm of the largest policeman with her fists; he grabbed her bodily and pushed her out of his way, where she overbalanced and fell, hauled to her feet by other women nearby.

"Oh, what's –" Lily clutched Polly's arm for support.

The crowd around them, orderly and still a few moments before, was now turbulent with crosscurrents. Polly felt panic rising. Never in her life had she been in the middle of such a crowd; never before had she feared being accidentally crushed or trampled. "They've come for Edwina!" she gasped to Lily. "She knew they would – she'll be taken back to prison –"

"Then why did she come? She didn't have to –"

Hemmed in on all sides, Polly tried to see what was happening. Only four policemen, in this crowd – so outnumbered, how could they succeed? But, glancing behind her, Polly saw another line of police by the Park Lane railings – reinforcements, intimidating, with their uniforms, helmets and truncheons. Only a few of the women were brave enough to attack the officers with fists or placards or, in one or two cases, with clubs they must have hidden under their skirts. More policemen shoved through to catch hold of these women and take them to the rear. Polly glimpsed one of them, kicking and shouting as a large policeman lifted her bodily off the ground.

"Girls, girls, come away, let's move back under the trees –" Aunt Dorothy was trying to reach them, grabbing Lily's sleeve. Lily moved toward her aunt, looking around for Polly, but Polly, anxious to see what had happened to Edwina, pretended not to notice.

"Excuse me – I've got to –" Gradually, ducking under elbows and between bodies, she made her way nearer to the speaker's platform. Abruptly the breath was slammed out of her lungs as someone lurched back and collided with her. Knocked sideways, she turned awkwardly and felt a wrench of pain in her right ankle. She was down, sprawled on the ground, clutching at someone's skirt as she fell; she glimpsed lace petticoats and dainty shoes, serge trousers and a policeman's heavy boots, then arms reached down and hoisted her upright. "Oops-a-daisy! Are you all right, my duck?" A kindly woman was brushing her down.

Polly nodded, her eyes filling with tears as the sickness of pain reeled through her. She put her right foot to the ground, found that it would still bear her weight – not broken, then, thank goodness! "Thank you," she managed, with a grimacing attempt at a smile, and limped forward.

Edwina carried on speaking into the megaphone until the very last moment. Polly saw her sway and stumble as she was pulled off the box, then handcuffs flashed as she was captured. Edwina did not struggle, did not even try to resist. She held her head high, surrounded by a flock of her closest followers as two policemen led her away toward a black van that waited on Park Lane.

It's what she wanted, Polly realized. She wanted to

be handcuffed and led away in full view of everyone. She knew this would happen. If she hadn't wanted it, she could have kept herself hidden.

Some of the women pursued the police van as it drove away, hammering on the roof with their fists, shouting at the policemen inside or with words of encouragement to Edwina. Others, rallied by Miss Selby, who now had the megaphone, were pressing back into Speaker's Corner.

What now? Miss Selby had righted the box and was standing on it, trying to restore order. "We have just seen an example of the Cat and Mouse Act in action," she yelled, "the Liberal government's way of dealing with political protestors! We must not allow this violent interruption to hinder our peaceful proceedings. The march will continue as planned." Gradually the hubbub faded, as she regained control of the throng. "Miss Rutherford, our brave comrade, was well aware that police would be waiting for her here. She helped plan the protest with this outcome in mind. She will endure another stay in prison with fortitude. Others are here to lead us to Chelsea Town Hall and to confront the Mayor and his party there. Proceed!" she finished dramatically, as if ordering a cavalry into battle.

Polly tested her ankle, hobbling a few steps. Though weakened and painful, it would bear her weight. Everyone was gradually moving and shuffling, marshaled by stewards, into Broad Walk. Polly could no longer see Aunt Dorothy or Lily; she thought they had moved back toward the railings. Deliberately she did not look around: if Aunt Dorothy saw that she was injured, there would be no question of marching even a short way. Having gotten this far, Polly was determined not to give up, even if the distance from here to Chelsea Town Hall now seemed a very long way indeed. She slipped into the column, surrounding herself with taller people.

Posters were held aloft, banners raised, purple, white and green, giving a festive air as the procession moved off. "Votes for women!" someone shouted at the front, and the cry was taken up by others. Progress was a slow shamble at first, almost treading on the heels of people in front, then accelerating to the brisk pace set by the stewards. At first, Polly's injured foot made her wince with each step, but the pain soon began to lessen.

"Get back to your kitchen sinks!" a passerby yelled from Park Lane.

"Should be locked up, the lot of you!" someone else shouted. And one of the marching women called back, "We will be, if that's what it costs!"

Polly felt herself bubbling inside with pride and excitement, willing to march for miles and miles. She would hop on one foot, if necessary! The taunters were on the other side of the railings; she was on this side, surrounded by strong-minded women. She would do it. Nothing would stop her now. She was marching with the suffragettes, and she felt that nothing in her life so far had been as worthwhile.

CHAPTER FOURTEEN

Caught

By the time the procession had passed through the park, and was moving down Sloane Street, it had attracted attention of various kinds. A group of boys ran up and down the length of the column, screaming taunts; someone threw a tomato, which burst squashily against one of the poster boards and left a juicy trail of seeds on the hats of the two nearest women; some bystanders laughed, or just turned to stare. But others applauded, or shouted, "Good luck to you!"

Polly had not seen Lily or Aunt Dorothy since the marchers had moved off. By now, she was trying to squash a feeling of guilty unease beneath her excitement. The urge to join the marchers had been so irresistible that she'd almost forgotten what she'd told Aunt Dorothy about just looking, or about walking only a little way. Where were they? Somewhere behind, she assumed – but they would be worried, having lost her in the scuffle at Speaker's Corner. How was she going to find them again? A woman walking beside her asked kindly, "Excuse me, my dear, but I can't help feeling anxious – are you all on your own? Is your mother not with you?"

"No," Polly replied; "I'm with my friend and her aunt. They're coming along behind."

"And you seem to be limping – have you blistered your foot, dear, with all this walking?"

Polly shook her head and shrugged off the sympathy,

but felt a little less alone. This woman was quite old, older than Polly's grandmother, with white hair and a lined face, but was striding out as purposefully as anyone.

In the King's Road, people came out of shops and stood in doorways to watch. The procession took up the width of the street, bringing traffic to a standstill. Whether Polly looked ahead or behind, all she could see was a mass of heads, beribboned hats, the banners proclaiming VOTES FOR WOMEN, and the placards bobbing like marker buoys in a harbor. At the Town Hall – the grand new building with its classical pillared entrances and its gilded clock – everything became a little confused. Everyone wanted to get as close to the steps as possible, but the helmeted heads of policemen could be seen above the crush of people, intent on keeping the roadway clear so that the Mayor and his guests could enter the building. Afraid of being knocked over again, Polly found a safe place to stand, on the corner of Chelsea Manor Street, which gave her a good view of the proceedings. It had been hot and tiring, walking in the heat; she felt sweat trickling inside her blouse, her feet unbearably hot, and now that she had stopped walking, her ankle was throbbing painfully enough to make her feel sick. Maybe she had injured it more badly than she thought after all, and all the walking was making it worse.

For the first time she saw Violet, with a group standing on the far side of the entrance. One of them held a large sealed letter, for the Mayor, Polly presumed. Of Lily and Aunt Dorothy there was no sign, but if they had been toward the back of the procession it would be difficult for them to get anywhere near the Town Hall steps.

Numbers of police now formed a semi-circular barricade to keep the entrance clear. Guests were starting to arrive, walking from taxicabs drawn up as close as they could get – gentlemen in tail coats and bow ties, and jeweled ladies in evening dresses, some wrapped in shawls in spite of the evening's warmth.

They picked their way carefully, guided by police; some gave disdainful looks at the mass of women. Polly saw that the kind white-haired woman who had spoken to her on the march had positioned herself close enough to the police cordon to reach out an arm and offer a leaflet to each person who approached the entrance. Most simply ignored her; one man accepted a leaflet and gave it a disparaging glance before crumpling it in his hand and tossing it to the ground. Only one of the guests, a gracious-looking woman in dark red with a tasseled silk wrap, took a leaflet and smiled her thanks before being guided up the steps by a policeman.

Polly knew that everyone was waiting for the Mayor himself – or was he already inside? She was hoping for a magnificently grand entrance. Maybe he would arrive in a carriage drawn by six black horses, and would be resplendent in scarlet, bedecked with chains of office. But now everything was happening at once. She saw Violet, with two other women, duck beneath the arms of the unsuspecting policemen to rush for the steps, Violet in the lead, holding the sealed letter. A stir of excitement rippled through the waiting crowd. The liveried footman at the door gave a yell, and a constable leaped up to tackle Violet from behind.

"Listen to our demands!" someone yelled, and more voices joined in with, "Votes for women!"

Another voice shrilled through the chanting. "Polly! Polly!" It was Aunt Dorothy, trying to move toward her from the other side of the police cordon; Polly glimpsed Lily's anxious face beside her, straining to see. Now more guests were arriving, two gentlemen and a woman; Violet and her two companions had been bundled to one side of the entrance. Polly stood undecided, while Aunt Dorothy called again, more urgently.

The new guests passed so close that she registered a waft of flowery perfume. The taller of the two men, dressed in dinner jacket and black tie like the others, stopped in astonishment before reaching the steps.

"*Polly!* What, in heaven's name –"

Polly's heart pounded; she swayed, and put a hand against the wall to steady herself. Of all people, she had not expected to see Papa.

CHAPTER FIFTEEN

Disgrace

When Papa was displeased, he seemed to Polly like a cold stranger. This time he was more than displeased; he was almost white with anger. And the person he was most angry with was Aunt Dorothy.

He had excused himself from the Mayor's reception and led Polly down the King's Road, hailing the first taxicab he saw. Aunt Dorothy hurried after them to explain, but all Papa said, tight-lipped and aloof, was:

"My wife and I entrusted you with the care of our daughter, and you brought her to this – this scrimmage. That's as much as I need to know. We will discuss this tomorrow."

What made it even worse was that Polly's ankle had now stiffened badly, after all the walking and then standing still, and she could barely hobble, supported by her father's arm. At home, there was more shock and dismay from Mama, a barrage of questions, and Polly was made to sit on the sofa with her ankle propped on a cushioned footstool, while Dr. Mayes was summoned, and Mrs. Parks fetched cold washcloths. Her injury at least protected her from the worst of Papa's wrath, but she could not hold back the hot tears that spilled down her cheeks. The dizzy excitement of earlier this evening had turned to this – pain, anger, difficult explanations.

"So," Papa persisted, "That Woman" (for this was what Aunt Dorothy had now become) "deliberately deceived us, led us to believe you were spending a quiet evening at her home with Lily, then led you into that street brawl?"

"No! It wasn't her fault!" Polly said hotly. "It was all my idea – I wanted to go, and I persuaded her to take us – and I promised to stay with her and not get into trouble –"

"Mrs. Langrish must take the blame, though, Polly," said Mama. "She was in charge of you, and Lily. I don't imagine Lily's parents will be at all pleased when they hear about it, either. It really was very irresponsible of Mrs. Langrish, when she must have known that neither we nor Lily's parents would have allowed it."

"It's utterly disgraceful!" Papa almost spat the words. "Your mother must find you another piano teacher, Polly – and I shall call tomorrow to tell That Woman exactly what I think of her conduct. I'm surprised she isn't more careful of her reputation."

"As for letting you tramp miles through the streets with a sprained ankle –" Mama bent to examine it again, shaking her head.

"She didn't! I didn't even tell her, and I set off ahead of her and Lily so that she wouldn't find out."

Papa's expression became even sterner. "So you were *unaccompanied* on the march? Polly, this is sounding worse and worse."

They were interrupted by the arrival of Dr. Mayes, who examined Polly's ankle, turning it this way and that, and asked her to wiggle her toes.

"Nothing broken," he pronounced. "But you've wrenched it badly. There will be bruising and swelling, nothing worse. Rest for you, young lady, until the swelling starts to subside, and cold compresses will help. I'd give her some hot, sweet tea now, for the shock," he added to Mama.

In bed at last, uncomfortably turning her ankle this way and that to avoid the pressure from the bedcovers, Polly realized that she had scarcely given a thought to Violet or Edwina. Edwina had been driven away in the van, presumably back to Holloway; but what of Violet, last seen in the grip of a policeman at the entrance to the Town Hall? Polly listened intently for any creak of floorboards from the apartment above, but heard nothing. How was she to find out? It would be no use asking Mama or Papa, and there was no chance of going upstairs. What if Violet had been arrested, too? And as for Lily – Polly had no idea how she was going to see Lily again, before she left for Tunbridge Wells. Her parents had made it clear that she wasn't going anywhere, not even downstairs for tea with Maurice. It would be awful for Lily's stay to end like this, without even the chance to say goodbye to each other.

In the morning her foot had stiffened so badly that she could only hop. She was excused from going to church, but her parents went as usual, leaving her in Mrs. Parks's charge. "You're not to move from this sofa," Mama instructed, handing her a prayer book. "And since you can't come with us, I suggest you spend the time reading this instead."

Polly was unable to concentrate on reading the prayer book or anything else. Smells of roasting meat drifted in from the kitchen, and she could hear Mrs. Parks humming as she worked, clattering pans, setting the table in the dining room. After gazing at a single page for some minutes without taking in a word of it, an idea occurred to her.

Still humming cheerfully in a way she would never do if Polly's parents were at home, Mrs. Parks entered the room with a glass of milk and a sugared cookie for Polly.

"Mrs. Parks," Polly asked, "do you ever talk to Kitty – you know, the maid upstairs?"

"Indeed I do," replied Mrs. Parks, plumping up the sofa cushions. "She's my niece."

"Your *niece!*"

It had never occurred to Polly to think about Mrs. Parks's family life. She was an indispensable part of the household, the person who made sure there was food in the pantry, meals on the table, and freshly laundered clothes to wear, and that was as far as Polly usually considered. Now that she thought about it, she had a vague idea that Mrs. Parks had a son, and presumably a husband.

"It was through me Kitty got that job," Mrs. Parks continued. "I knew the young ladies was looking for a maid-housekeeper, and I thought it would suit Kitty, so I spoke to them about her. She's very happy with them. Now, I must start cooking the vegetables, or there won't be any dinner."

All these lives going on, Polly thought, so close to her own, yet she knew so little about them! "Mrs. Parks," she said, "can you do something for me? Can you find out from Kitty what happened to Violet and Edwina yesterday? I don't know if Violet's come home – whether she's –"

Mrs. Parks glanced out of the open window. "Here's your ma and pa now, with the Dalbys – I must get on. Yes, all right, Miss Polly," she added in a low voice. "I'll do my best."

Polly picked up the prayer book, arranged herself demurely on the sofa and pretended to be absorbed in reading. It would take a few moments for Mama and Papa to go around to the side entrance and up the stairs. While she composed herself, she heard loud voices in the front garden: several of them, voices raised in dispute, and one that sounded like Lily's. She swung herself off the sofa and limped painfully to the window.

Her parents, with Mr. and Mrs. Dalby and Maurice, were inside the wrought-iron gates; they must be going in with the Dalbys, as they occasionally did, for a glass of sherry. Outside, trying to come through, were Aunt Dorothy and Lily. Papa had pushed the gates closed.

"I will not allow it!" Tall, haughty, he barred the way. "Please leave the premises. Polly is not well enough for visitors, and I don't want her to see Lily again during her stay. That is to be her punishment."

"O-oh!" Lily wailed. "Please let me come in, only for a few minutes! I'm going home today, and it's my last chance!"

"I have said no, Lily, and no is what I mean. I have no intention of arguing about it in the public street."

"We only wanted to see how she is, and bring her bag back!" Aunt Dorothy tried.

Papa reached for the bag. "Thank you," he said coldly; then closed and latched the gates. "Mrs. Langrish, I give you notice that we will be finding another piano teacher for Polly. I have forbidden her to return to Wellington Square. Good day."

Mama hadn't said a word. She followed Papa as he turned toward the door, following the Dalbys. Aunt Dorothy and Lily stood for a few moments, looking at them over the fence; then, as Polly watched, they turned away.

Polly opened the window wider. "Lily!" she shouted.

Lily stopped and looked around; Polly saw that she was crying.

"*Polly!*" Papa turned to face the second-floor window, his face rigid with anger. "Close that window at once!"

"I'll write to you!" Polly yelled to Lily.

"Did you hear me, young madam!" Papa wasn't shouting; he spoke in what was almost a stage whisper, but Polly heard him clearly enough.

"Best do what your pa says, lovey," said Mrs. Parks's quiet voice behind her. "You don't want to go asking for even more trouble."

CHAPTER SIXTEEN

Seaside Vacation

Polly was bored with staying indoors. She had been forbidden to go out, partly because of her swollen ankle, partly as punishment; and of course Papa was even crosser with her, now that she had defied him by shouting from the window. She played the piano, badly and half-heartedly; she wrote a letter to Aunt Dorothy to say she was sorry, and one to Lily, and asked Maurice to mail them for her in secret. No one came to see her, apart from Maurice; no Lily, no Aunt Dorothy, and no chance at all of speaking to Violet. Lily had gone back to Tunbridge Wells, leaving Polly with no idea when she was ever going to see her again. Everything had gone dull and flat since the march. And, as Mrs. Parks reminded her, the suffragettes had been campaigning for years for the vote; why should they succeed now?

Wasn't it exciting, though? Lily wrote from Tunbridge Wells. *Even if we did get into trouble. Even if you did go marching off on your own and didn't even wait for me, which was rather bad of you, frankly. But I will be generous and believe that you were overwhelmed by the occasion. Your papa was really quite beastly about it, but my mother says she will write to him herself and tell him that it was partly my fault for persuading Aunt Dorothy, and she thinks that if she asks really nicely he will relent and let you come and stay with us for two weeks later on. He and your mother will be completely taken up with the new baby, Mama says, so they will be glad to have you off their hands.*

The thought of the new baby taking up everyone's attention did little to improve Polly's mood. Bored, hot and sulky, she looked out of the dining-room window. Even the garden looked past its best: wilting in the heat, the roses dropping faded petals, the grass browning. Preparations were now being made for Folkestone – clothes sorted, trunks packed – but Polly could not even look forward to that, very much. Her parents' disapproval had now reached a third stage. Their first reaction had been concern for her injury, their anger directed at Aunt Dorothy; after Dr. Mayes's visit, Polly herself had received the full blast of her father's disapproval, in the form of several lectures on disobedience and its consequences. Now, that phase was over, and it seemed to be agreed that Polly's misdemeanor would never be mentioned again, but there was a chilly politeness in the air that was almost worse than being punished.

The only good thing was that Mrs. Parks had kept her promise by finding out what had happened to Violet. In response to Kitty's inquiries, Violet sent a note, which Polly kept hidden in her handkerchief drawer. She had written:

Dear Polly,

I am so sorry to hear you have hurt your ankle. Consider it an honorable injury. We were very pleased with the numbers attending our march, and very grateful to you for coming, even though it turned out badly for you. Although we did not gain admittance to the Town Hall, I did give my letter and petition to an official who promised me he would deliver it personally to the Lord Mayor. Edwina, as you probably saw, was re-arrested and taken back to Holloway, where I shall visit her as soon as it is allowed. I am sure she will resume her hunger strike and will be released when the prison authorities think she is too weak to continue.

We are so grateful for your support, Polly, as I know it is difficult for you. If I can see a chance of speaking to you in the garden, I will come down; if not I can send you notes through Kitty to let you know when Edwina is home. I hope your ankle heals quickly and that you have an enjoyable stay at Folkestone. Do let me know when you return.

With sincerest good wishes,
Your friend,
Violet Cross

Polly showed the letter to Maurice, who had become, oddly, a sort of ally. He was rather impressed by the way Polly had contrived to go on the march, and by Edwina's arrest.

"Did they really put handcuffs on her, and haul her off to the van?"

"Yes – and Violet could easily have gotten herself arrested, too," Polly told him. "Not for doing anything bad, like attacking someone – just for trying to give a petition to the Lord Mayor!"

"My mother's written another letter to the Earl of Belmont, to say those two shouldn't be allowed to live here. He answered her first one, but didn't say he was going to do anything about it."

Polly looked at him. "Did you hope he would? Did you think he'd turn up here and throw them out onto the street?"

"'Course not. Well," Maurice conceded, "I might have hoped for that at first, but now I think it's interesting, having them here. I'd be sorry if they left. What if Edwina dies? How many times can you starve yourself?"

"I don't know." Polly was unsure whether hunger striking would get easier each time, or harder.

Meanwhile, her parents were behaving as if Edwina and Violet simply didn't exist; as if it would be shameful even to mention them. Maurice and Polly agreed that it was quite ridiculous, the way grownups behaved sometimes. Polly trusted Maurice, by now, not to tell his mother about Violet's letter. It was fun, sharing secrets. With Lily gone, Maurice would have to do.

"You might send me a postcard from the seaside," Maurice said, "and bring me back a stick of rock."

"Yes, all right."

"Make sure you get back before the war starts," Maurice warned.

"You and your war!" Polly teased. "You'll be disappointed if it all comes to nothing! Go and play with your soldiers."

"It won't," Maurice said. "You only have to look at the newspapers."

In Folkestone there would not even be Maurice, and although there would be sea and sand, Polly did not see how she was going to enjoy them much, on her own, unable to walk far, and with Mama resting each afternoon. If only Lily could come!

London was so hot and dusty that Polly began to think longingly of rain and fog, of winter nights and drawn curtains, of frost patterns on the windowpanes. It was a relief, at last, to be on the train to Folkestone, looking out at meadows and hills, woods and cornfields and orchards, oast houses with their pointy white hats that Papa said were called cowls, and the sweep of the North Downs. Mama sat fanning herself, half dozing; occasionally her head would nod with sleep till she blinked awake again to gaze uncomprehendingly out of the window. Polly had started a new book, *Little Women*, given to her by Mama. She had finished *Under Desert Skies*, and would have preferred to choose something else from Edwina's crammed bookshelves, but as that was impossible she was reading Mama's choice. She had expected it to be all about girls behaving nicely, and indeed Meg and Beth always did, but she found an unexpected fictional ally in spirited Jo. With her ambition to be an author, Jo was a character Edwina would approve of.

Papa was engrossed in *The Times*. The front page was full of news about armies mobilizing, and ultimatums.

"Papa," Polly asked, "what's an ultimatum, please?"

He lowered the newspaper. "It's a final demand. It means giving someone a last chance to do something, or face reprisals."

"What are reprisals?"

"Reprisals are – well, a sort of punishment. The consequences of doing something, or of not doing something." He gave her a significant look.

"Is there going to be a war?" Polly asked, not wanting the conversation to take a personal turn.

"Oh, it's not settled yet," said Papa, in his *wait-and-see* voice.

At Folkestone they settled themselves into a boarding house on the seafront. The other family staying there had two children much younger than Polly, to her disappointment, and their own nursemaid to look after them. There were strolls along the promenade, a band concert, and on one afternoon a troupe of jugglers and acrobats in the park. Best of all, there was the sea. Polly never tired of it: the ever-changing light, the saltiness on her lips and in her hair, the mesmerizing sound of the waves, the crunch of stones as the undertow sucked back. The gulls screamed with a sound that was at once restless and soothing. She could see ships far out in the Channel, and sometimes, hazily, the coast of France. How odd that it was so near: nearer, Papa said, than home was.

There were soldiers, too, in Folkestone, marching to or from nearby barracks in their khaki uniforms, accompanied by officers on horseback. Polly thought of Maurice. GERMANY DECLARES WAR ON FRANCE was all over the newspaper billboards, in big letters.

Papa went out early each morning to buy his copy of *The Times*, and would not go to the promenade or beach till he had read it.

"If there's war between Germany and France, will we be in it?" Polly asked him.

"Well, you see, we're part of a treaty that says Belgium is neutral. If Germany invades Belgium we'll be drawn into the conflict."

It was like a new language, all this talk of alliances and mobilizations, of pacts and treaties. But the day after the Bank Holiday Monday, all the wondering was answered by one simple word: WAR.

CHAPTER SEVENTEEN

Ends and Beginnings

The vacation was over, though it had hardly begun. "We must go home," Mama kept saying, growing more agitated every time she glanced at the newspaper, or looked out of the window. "I don't feel safe here. I want us all to be at home."

Papa, too, decided that he was needed urgently at work, since the outbreak of war affected banking in ways Polly didn't understand. "We'll go tomorrow.

We'll pack up as quickly as we can, and I'll arrange train tickets."

"We're so vulnerable here." Mama could not sit still; she kept looking out at the promenade, then lowering herself into a chair, only to struggle up again a moment later. "Suppose the Germans invade? Supposing the baby's born here, with a German army in control?"

"Catherine, please!" Papa guided her back to her seat, and handed her a glass of water. "Don't alarm yourself unnecessarily – it won't do you any good. We'll be back at home this time tomorrow. I can't see any German invaders at the moment."

He spoke flippantly, but Polly glanced out at the shining strip of sea that was visible from their second-floor room, imagining the Germans rising out of the waves, as if they had swum all the way underwater. She had never seen a German. What would they look like? She imagined them as pirates boarding a captive ship, bloodthirsty and fierce, clamping knives between their teeth. And the captive ship would be England.

All the clothes so recently unpacked were refolded and stored back in their trunks. The station was full of khaki and backpacks and men's deep voices; a train full of soldiers had just arrived. At a command from their officer, all the men shouldered their packs and fell into line, moving off toward the harbor; they would be going across to France, Papa said. There were cheers from the street at the sight of the soldiers in uniform, and some people waved Union flags. The atmosphere, Polly thought, was partly of celebration, partly of waiting for something to happen. A second trainload pulled in while she waited with her parents on the platform. It felt odd to be traveling in the other direction, as if they were running away from the war, while everyone else was rushing toward it.

Half an hour later she was staring out of the train window again, in a hot compartment that smelled of dust and hot cushions, and seeing all the Kent scenery again – the drowsing orchards, the grazing sheep, the oast houses. The stuffiness made her drift off. When she snapped back awake it was to find Mama slumping sideways on her seat, and Papa bending over her in concern.

"Open the window, Polly, quickly. It's the heat – she's passed out."

He unbuttoned the cuffs of Mama's blouse, and took off his jacket to use as a pillow, lowering her to a half-lying position. Polly struggled with the window and managed to push it down so that smutty air rushed into the compartment. Mama murmured, but her eyelids stayed closed.

"Is she ill, Papa? Will she die?" Polly's voice came out very small and frightened.

"No, no, of course not. It's the heat, and the rush and excitement. We must get her home as quickly as we can – call Dr. Mayes –"

"Is it the baby? Is the baby coming early?" Polly was rather vague about how exactly babies were born, but could see that it would take something very extraordinary to get it out of Mama and into the world as a separate human being.

"I hope not," Papa said fervently. Polly saw that he too was scared, and did not really know what to do. This in itself was so alarming that Polly felt herself trembling, close to tears.

"There's a flask of water in that traveling bag. Fetch it, please, there's a good girl." Papa was holding one of Mama's hands, and seemed unwilling to let go. "Then I want you to go along to the guard's van and explain that Mama is unwell. He can summon help when we arrive at Victoria Station."

By the time Polly got back from finding the guard, Mama had revived a little, enough to sit up and sip water as the familiar London buildings slid into view, and the train crossed the Thames before slowing for the terminus. At Victoria Station, the guard summoned a cab and supervised the loading of the luggage, while Polly's father helped Mama into her seat. More crowds packed the station: soldiers in uniform, nurses, families waving them off.

Home had never seemed so welcoming: the house solid and calm behind its gates, Mrs. Parks in charge, everything in order. It felt to Polly as if she had never been away. Her father helped Mama to bed, and Mrs. Parks fetched cool drinks and a cold compress, while Polly tried to make herself useful by starting to unpack. Dr. Mayes arrived, and there was a hushed conference in the bedroom, while Polly hovered uncertainly outside the door.

"Baby's on its way," Mrs. Parks told Polly when she emerged. "A bit early, but Doctor thinks all will be well. I must boil up some hot water, and we'll need washcloths, and clean towels."

"I'll fetch them," Polly offered, but at the same moment her father came out of the bedroom, looking both eager and anxious.

"Polly, I want you to go downstairs to Mrs. Dalby, and stay there till I come and fetch you. I saw Maurice in the garden – you can go and play with him if you like."

"But –" Polly felt herself too grownup for playing, too important to be simply gotten rid of. She had helped on the train, hadn't she, and at the station, with the cab and the luggage?

"Go," said her father firmly. "You'll only be in everyone's way. Your mother will be perfectly all right with Dr. Mayes to look after her. I'll come and fetch you as soon as there's any news."

"It's best you do as he says," Mrs. Parks told her in an undertone. "You go and see Maurice. Before long, you'll have a little brother or sister – won't that be exciting? And" – she checked that Papa had gone back into the bedroom, and that the door was closed – "there's news from upstairs. Miss Rutherford's back from prison, but apparently Miss Cross is moving out!"

"Moving out? Why?"

"Some argument, Kitty said. Now, you run along." Mrs. Parks shooed Polly toward the stairs.

Polly closed the door to the apartment but stood on the landing, listening. Floorboards creaked from the apartment above, and she heard a voice call out – Violet's? It seemed an age since she'd had any sort of proper conversation with Violet or Edwina. No one was going to take much notice of where she was, not with everyone scurrying about with compresses and towels and hot water. She went upstairs instead of down, then hesitated again at the door of Apartment Three. An argument, Mrs. Parks had said? Like last time? But the voice she'd just heard didn't sound like arguing; it only sounded like Violet calling out to Edwina, in a perfectly cheerful way.

While she stood there, the door opened and Kitty came out, almost colliding with her. "Oh! I'm sorry. Do come in. We're all in a muddle."

Kitty stepped aside for Polly to enter. A suitcase stood in the hall with an umbrella leaning against it, and a leather traveling bag, and two small packing crates. It was true, then, what Mrs. Parks had said.

"You can keep all them posters," Violet's voice called out, "but I'm taking my banner, seeing as I wore out my fingers sewing it – oh! Polly! Thought you was at Folkestone?"

"We're back because of the war," Polly explained, "and now Mama's having the baby. The doctor's with her now. But what's happening here? Why are you leaving? It's not Mrs. Dalby, is it?"

Violet looked puzzled. "Mrs. Dalby?"

"Maurice's mother. She thought –" Polly felt awkward saying it. "She thought you and Edwina shouldn't be allowed to live here."

"Oh!" Violet seemed to think this of no consequence whatsoever. "No, no, it en't that. Come and say hello to Edwina. She's been ill again, but getting better."

Edwina was at her desk in the drawing room, sorting through papers. She looked just as thin and frail as when Polly had first met her: how could she keep on *doing* this to herself? Polly wondered.

"They let us all out of prison, because of the war,"

she told Polly. "So I can eat again, hoorah! And Kitty's made us a lovely cherry cake. Do stay and share it with us."

Polly was puzzled – there seemed to be no sign of another quarrel, yet it seemed that Violet was leaving, and Edwina was staying. She was halfway through her slice of cake before she plucked up the courage to ask them about it. They exchanged rueful glances in the way Polly had seen before. Then Edwina replied:

"Well, Polly, you've obviously realized that Violet and I, though the best of friends, don't always see eye to eye. And especially so, now that war's broken out. The Pankhursts have split over it, and so have we. We feel quite differently about the war, and what it means for our aims. Mrs. Pankhurst has decided that all our campaigning must stop – we must support enlistment, encourage men to join the army. And besides that, we'll work, we'll work hard, whatever way we can, so the government will see just what women can do when they're given the chance. I'm going to be a volunteer nurse, and get out to France or Belgium if I can. Whereas –" She nodded to Violet, who took over.

"Back to the East End, for me. It's where I belong, and where I should be now." She smiled. "I've liked living here, and I've liked meeting you, Polly, but now I'm going back, to work with Sylvia Pankhurst. Her aims have always been a bit different from her mother's and Christabel's. Sylvia's against the war, like I am. And it's the poor that's going to suffer most, like always. She wants to help the East End families – they'll be facing a real struggle, with their men away. And that's where I'm going, too, to work in a canteen. There's so much to be done."

"Oh." Polly looked from one to the other, with the sad sense that something was coming to an end: the specialness contained in this apartment, and all it had meant to her. Edwina would still be here, but it wouldn't be the same without Violet.

Violet was looking wistful, too. She reached for an old envelope from the heap of papers Edwina was sorting. "Here, I'll give you my address. Maybe you'll write?"

"Of course I will," Polly said. "And –?" She looked at Edwina.

"Oh, we'll still stay friends, Violet and I," Edwina said. "We've known each other too long to fall out completely over a difference of opinion. And we haven't gotten votes for women yet! Till then, there's a lot more campaigning to do."

Violet handed Polly the envelope: on it she had written *c/o Miss Sylvia Pankhurst, 400 Old Ford Road, London, E.3.* She glanced at the clock. "Time to be on my way." She stood, and shook hands formally with Polly.

"Goodbye, Violet," Polly said. "I – I'm sorry."

"So am I," Violet replied. "About this sorry mess those politicians have got us into. But sorry to be saying goodbye, Polly, too. It's been nice getting to know you a bit. Good luck to you. I hope you do whatever you want in your life."

"Get the vote," Edwina said. "And know what you want to do – be an explorer. Do it. Decide for yourself."

They were in agreement about *that*, anyway.

Feeling slightly dazed by it all, Polly wandered out into the garden. Everything was changing, she thought, and by the time she went back upstairs her family would have changed, too. There would be herself, Mama, Papa, and someone else: this unknown new person, with a whole life to live. What a strange thought that was!

"Hello, Pegs," Maurice called. Funny, but she didn't mind anymore when he called her that; it sounded friendly now. He was standing underneath the walnut tree, looking up into its branches. "Look, you can see the new walnuts coming. We'll be able to eat them at Christmas."

Polly looked at the small green fruits in the lushness of leaves high above her head. She thought of the girl who had lived here, long ago, who had grown this whole tree from one walnut. Could she have ever imagined, carefully planting one shriveled walnut in the soil, two children standing in its shade, looking up at its new crop of nuts?

"Isn't it exciting about the war?" Maurice said, turning to look at her. "You can join the army at eighteen, so I've only got five years and ten months to wait. If I go into the army I shall be an officer."

"Don't be stupid," Polly said, laughing. "The war's not going to go on for five years and ten months, is it? Everyone says it'll be over by Christmas."

CHAPTER EIGHTEEN

Secrets

Dear Lily, Polly wrote. *So much has happened since I sent you the postcard from Folkestone that I hardly know where to start. Most exciting of all is that I have a brand new baby brother! He was born yesterday and his name is Edward. Till a few weeks ago Mama and Papa had thought of calling him William if he turned out to be a boy, but now of course they can't, because of Kaiser Wilhelm. So he is named Edward after the old King.*

All the waiting time I was hoping he would be a girl, but after all I am quite pleased to have a brother.

Polly had not realized this until writing it down. It was another of the surprising changes that yesterday had brought.

The baby had taken so long being born that Polly had stayed for supper with the Dalbys and played two games of chess with Maurice on the landing, losing both times, because Maurice was rather good at chess. "It's like war," he told her. "All about maneuvers and stealth."

It was almost bedtime before Mrs. Parks came down with the news. "You've got a new baby brother! Come up and meet him!"

"A boy! Oh, what wonderful news!" Mrs. Dalby clapped her hands. "There, didn't I tell you it would be a boy? Your father will be so delighted!"

But Polly, not delighted at all, had felt a lump of

sourness inside her as she climbed the stairs as slowly as she could – a lump that stuck in her throat and would hardly let her swallow.

"Come along!" Mrs. Parks urged, as if the new baby were already so important that he mustn't be kept waiting five minutes.

In the bedroom, Mama smiled wearily from her propped-up pillows. "Here he is! Come and see." She was holding a white bundle that looked too tiny to be a baby. Polly bent over to look, and saw a small red face bunched up tightly, an almost cross expression, and a hand with tiny, tiny fingernails.

"Oh!" She couldn't help it; she heard the adoring note in her voice she had heard other people use when they looked at babies.

Papa was sitting in a chair beside the bed. "Meet your big sister!" he told the baby, in a funny, crooning voice Polly couldn't remember him ever using before. "She's going to be a very important person in your life."

Mama reached up her spare hand to pull Polly

toward her for a kiss and a one-armed hug. "He's a very lucky baby, to have the best sister in the world! Would you like to hold him?"

He is so beautiful, Polly wrote. *Have you ever held a new baby? I hadn't, and it was amazing. He is so little and so light to hold, but then he wriggled and I could feel how strong and alive he is. His eyes are open but he doesn't even know how to see things yet. Isn't it amazing to think of all the things he will have to learn?*

Mama gave a tired smile, settling her head comfortably against the pillows. "Thank you, darling."

"What for?" Polly couldn't think of anything that deserved thanks.

"For being so good." Mama tried to stifle a yawn. "So helpful and considerate. You know you really can be such a good girl, when you want to be."

Well, yes. It was funny, Polly thought, how grownups sometimes said what was not quite what they meant, but was truer than what they'd intended to say. Yes, when I want to be; but that isn't always.

"What is it, Polly?" said Mama, who was sometimes very good at knowing when Polly was hiding something. Papa had gone into the drawing room to start writing cards to all the relations with news of the baby's arrival.

"It's – well, I –" Polly did not know how to put it, but came straight out with, "I expect you and Papa are very pleased to have a boy, because you'd have been disappointed if it had been another girl, wouldn't you?" It sounded like an accusation. "I mean, everyone says, at least Mrs. Dalby does, that a boy would be best."

"Polly! Is that what you've been worrying about?" Mama said gently. "Yes, we're delighted to have a boy, because now we're very lucky to have a son *and* a lovely daughter. But you mustn't ever think we love one of you more than the other! Promise me you will never believe that?"

"The way Papa talked to the baby just now!" Polly said, to avoid answering. "I don't believe he ever talked to me like that!"

"Polly," Mama said firmly. "When you were born, your father was the proudest man in London. He told me he felt as if he could leap the River Thames in one bound or jump up and swing from the hands of Big Ben. And he still is, Polly – as proud of his daughter as I am."

Mama and I have a secret, now, Polly wrote. *I didn't think Mama ever had secrets from Papa, but she does, and this is it.*

"He gets such an unfair start, being a boy!" Now that Polly had started, something seemed to be pushing her to say more and more, all the things she had kept inside for so long. "I'm only a girl, so I have to be ladylike, and do what I'm told, and behave nicely, and have other people decide for me. He's only just born, but he'll be able to vote when he's grownup, and boss people about, and think himself better than me!"

"But, Polly, darling!" Mama rocked the baby gently in her arms. "Things are changing now, for women especially. You'll have the vote when you're old enough, I'm certain – thanks to the efforts of people like Miss Rutherford and Miss Cross, and their determination –"

"Mama!" Polly was astonished. "I thought you disapproved of them!"

Mama smiled. "I disapprove of some of the things they do. Your father disapproves of them, certainly. But –" She glanced at the closed door. "Perhaps this had better be our secret, Polly. I also admire them. I admire them for standing up for what they believe in, and for fighting for it. They are so brave, so determined not to give in! I could never do that myself, but I'm very glad there are people who do."

So, who would have guessed it? My mother a secret suffragette sympathizer! And now that we've got one secret, we can have more – that I shall write to Violet in the Old Ford Road, and even go to visit if I can. I have written her new address in the marbled notebook you gave me, which I use for my Plans and Ideas. My Plans and Ideas will have to be secret, but I will share them with you.

Papa sets the rules of the house, but he cannot tell me what to think. Mama always does what he says, because he is her husband and she promised to obey him and that is what everyone expects. But things are changing, even Mama says so. Things will be different when we grow up. I'm going to be an explorer, and by then I expect women will be able to do all sorts of things they don't do now. Papa will have to get used to it.

He is so pleased and relieved about the baby, and that Mama is recovering well, that she thinks if I explain to him again about Hyde Park, and make him understand that it really was all my idea, not yours or Aunt Dorothy's, he will change his mind about the piano lessons, and will let me come to stay with you. Except now of course there's the war and that changes things again, because who knows what will happen? Maybe I'll be allowed to be friends with Edwina, too, now that she's giving up campaigning, to support the war effort. Papa can't object to that, can he?

So for now I shall have to make do with Maurice. But that's another strange thing – I have decided that Maurice isn't so bad after all, even if he does always beat me at chess. I think I will have to be truthful and say that I _like_ him.

Isn't it amazing how people can keep surprising you?

Author's Note

A hundred years ago, in 1918, women in Britain voted for the very first time. It had taken years of struggle, and even then not all women were allowed to vote – only those over thirty who owned houses or were graduates. It was another ten years before all women over twenty-one could vote on the same terms as men.

The campaign for Votes for Women was long and hard, and had been going on for years at the time of my story. There were various groups and societies, with differing ideas about how best to make their views known. Should they take part only in peaceful campaigning, petitioning, writing letters to MPs and so on – or should they use direct action, such as damaging property, starting fires and breaking into the Houses of Parliament? Many women were ready to put their lives at risk by going on a hunger strike in prison and starving themselves almost to death – and many went through the torture of force-feeding, not once but many times. How brave they must have been to face that!

This campaign was never going to be defeated, but perhaps it took the First World War (1914-18) for women to prove their worth to the country. While the fighting took place, women did all sorts of war work – driving ambulances, nursing, farming, working in factories and more. The war ended in November 1918 and that same month the law was changed, a first step toward equality.

Whenever there's an election and I go along to cast my vote, I think of the women (and some men) who fought so fiercely for my right to do so – women like Violet and Edwina.

Linda Newbery

About the Author

Linda has written many books for children, teenagers and adults. She won the Costa Children's Book Prize for *Set in Stone*, and has twice been shortlisted for the Carnegie Medal. With Yvonne Coppard she has written *Writing Children's Fiction: a Writers' and Artists' Companion*, and she runs a review blog, *Writers Review*, with Adèle Geras and Celia Rees, and help from many of their writer friends (including Ann Turnbull).

Linda lives in a small village in Oxfordshire and loves yoga, wildlife, photography, gardening and reading.

See more at *www.lindanewbery.co.uk*

USBORNE QUICKLINKS

For links to websites where you can find out more about the suffragette movement and other historical events in this book, go to the Usborne Quicklinks website at **www.usborne.com/quicklinks** and type in the title of this book.

At Usborne Quicklinks you can:

- Watch newsreels of suffragette processions
- Meet some of the suffragettes mentioned in the book
- Learn about female explorers of the day
- Find out more about everyday life in the early 1900s

Please follow the online safety guidelines at the Usborne Quicklinks website.